SWAN IN THE SWIM

'Mrs Parker Smythe!' Mandy interrupted urgently. '*What* is swimming in your pool?'

'A swan! An enormous, dangerous-looking swan! It's swimming in my beautiful pool! Are you sending your parents to Beacon House? You do realise this is an emergency! My house guests—'

'Someone will be there as soon as possible!' said Mandy, putting the receiver down and cutting Mrs Parker Smythe off in mid-flow. She quickly punched out the number of her mum's mobile phone. There was no reply.

What was she going to do now?

LUCY DANIELS

Swan
— *in the* —
Swim

Illustrations by Jenny Gregory

Hodder
Children's
Books

a division of Hodder Headline plc

Special thanks to Pat Posner
Thanks also to C. J. Hall, B.Vet.Med., M.R.C.V.S., for reviewing
the veterinary material contained in this book.

Text copyright © 1997 Ben M. Baglio
Created by Ben M. Baglio, London W6 0HE
Illustrations copyright © 1997 Jenny Gregory

First published in Great Britain in 1997
by Hodder Children's Books

A Catalogue record for this book is available from the British Library

ISBN 0 340 68717 7

Typeset by Avon Dataset Ltd, Bidford-on-Avon, Warks

Printed and bound in Great Britain by
Caledonian International Book Manufacturing Ltd, Glasgow

Hodder Children's Books
a division of Hodder Headline plc
338 Euston Road
London NW1 3BH

One

Mandy Hope glanced round and suddenly felt very nervous. Welford's village hall was packed. It seemed as though nearly everyone from the village, and quite a few from the outlying farms, wanted to hear and discuss the latest ideas for helping Welford to be chosen as the 'Friendliest Village' in North Yorkshire.

The competition had been launched by *Dales News*, the local evening newspaper. The response had been tremendous. Welford was competing against eleven other villages for the title. As well as points being awarded for friendliness, appearance and atmosphere, every village taking part in the competition was to revive the old tradition of rushbearing and build a rushcart.

Rushcart! Mandy's toes curled and she turned to look at her best friend, James Hunter. They had an idea for the rushcart. A brilliant idea! Something that none of the other villages would think of doing.

Mandy took a deep breath. Soon, she and James would be going up on to the platform to put their idea forward.

'Reverend Hadcroft likes our plan, Mandy,' said James. 'And Dan Venables is willing to lend us Duke. That's sure to help, you know!'

'Yes, it is,' she agreed. 'But—' Mandy broke off to look round the crowded hall again.

'Everyone knows you because of Animal Ark,' James added. 'That should help, as well.'

Mandy nodded. Her parents were Welford's vets. Animal Ark was the name of their veterinary practice. Animals were the love of Mandy's life; she wanted to be a vet, too, and often helped her mum and dad in the surgery.

'You're right, James,' said Mandy. 'It should help. I just hope everyone will vote in favour of our idea.'

'We'll soon find out,' said James, his eyes on the platform just in front of them where the village committee members were sitting. 'They're ready to start!'

A hush fell over the hall as Robert Markham, the committee secretary, rose to his feet. He declared the meeting open, read the minutes from the previous meeting, then asked the chairperson, Eileen Davy, to announce the evening's agenda.

Miss Davy rose to her feet, gave a sharp nod of her head, then began. 'First: Mandy Hope and James Hunter, second . . .'

Mandy gasped and stopped listening. She and James were first! She hadn't been expecting that. She heard James clear his throat; saw his hand move to push his glasses further on to his nose. James hadn't been expecting it either!

'Mandy, I've forgotten what I'm supposed to say,' he whispered.

'You'll remember when I start to talk,' Mandy whispered back, hoping she could remember her own words!

To Mandy's surprise, as the two of them walked up the steps to the platform, a few people in the hall started clapping. 'See,' said James, suddenly feeling a bit better, 'they're on our side already!'

Even Miss Davy, when she banged on the table

for silence, seemed to be smiling.

Then Mandy spoke into the silence. 'Last week, James and I were talking to Mrs Schofield, the librarian on the travelling library van. She told us that most of the villages taking part in the competition are going to have morris dancers or musicians following their rushcarts as part of the rushbearing procession.'

Mandy paused for a second to let that bit of news sink in, then she went on, 'Mrs Schofield showed us some old photos of rushcart processions and there were morris dancers or musicians in every one.' Mandy looked at James and nodded.

James gulped, took a couple of steps forward and said firmly, 'Somehow, that made it seem like we're only *half* doing things. There'll be points awarded for the rushcart procession and . . . and the other villages are doing more than we are!'

There was a murmur of agreement and Mandy smiled. James had got that over really well! Now it was her turn again. She decided to come straight to the point.

'Why don't we have a procession of animals following our rushcart?' she asked. 'Ending in a special animal service outside the church!'

'We're talking about pets *and* farm animals,' said James, before anyone had time to comment. 'Mr Venables is willing for Duke, his shire horse, to pull the rushcart.'

'And animals are just as much part of the village as *we* are!' Mandy added quickly.

She looked down at the sea of faces, trying to judge reactions. Everyone, apart from her dad and the vicar, looked as though they'd been turned to stone. Mandy's heart sank. *Didn't they like the idea at all, then . . . ?*

'I say good for the youngsters!' shouted old Walter Pickard, jumping to his feet. 'Their idea will give everyone a chance to help Welford win the title!'

'I second that!' his neighbour, Ernie Bell, said loudly.

A loud clapping and a few cheers then resounded round the hall. Mandy felt tears pricking the back of her eyes. Fancy down-to-earth Walter Pickard and Ernie Bell, who usually needed loads of time to think anything over, being the first ones to voice approval. They were both quite set in their ways, but highly regarded by everyone in the village.

As the clapping died down, Walter's young grandson, Tommy Pickard, said in a loud and puzzled voice, 'But what *is* a rushcart? Why does it go to the church?'

Everyone sitting near Tommy started to answer his questions at once: 'In the olden days, churches were cold and damp places with mud floors,' said Reverend Hadcroft. 'Rushes were used to try and keep the floors clean and to give a bit of warmth.'

'Lots of rushes were needed for the job,' added Lydia Fawcett. 'They were picked and left to dry then made into shapes or bundles. Then carts were used to carry the bundles to the churches.'

'So the carts came to be called rushcarts,' Reverand Hadcroft continued. 'The villagers followed their own cart to the church, dancing and singing. Then a church service was held to give thanks for the rushes.'

While all this was going on, Mandy sighed and looked despairingly at James. Surely someone would call for order soon and get back to their idea!

Mandy glanced to where the committee members were sitting. They were talking quietly amongst themselves, nodding and smiling. But then she saw Mr Markham saying something to Miss Davy. Miss Davy shook her head, and they both looked over to her and James.

'James,' Mandy muttered urgently, 'I've got a feeling Mr Markham isn't too happy about something!'

At last, Eileen Davy hammered for silence. She looked at Mandy and said, 'Have you and James sought Reverend Hadcroft's approval for your idea of a special service for the animals, Mandy?'

'Yes, they have!' The young vicar was on his feet and answering before Mandy could reply. 'And I'd just like to say that I think it's the nicest idea I've heard in a long time.'

'Thank you, Reverend Hadcroft. Now, is there anyone against?' Eileen Davy asked briskly.

'I'm not against exactly,' Mrs McFarlane, who ran the village post office, called out. 'But if it's a traditional to have dancers and suchlike, shouldn't *we* stick to tradition? Surely someone in the village could get a few dancers together and teach them the appropriate dance steps in time for the procession?'

Mandy held her breath and stared ahead to where Mrs Ponsonby was sitting. Bossy Mrs Ponsonby liked to think she was the only one who could organise anything in Welford. She'd be in her element giving dancing lessons! But

Mrs Ponsonby's head was bowed; all Mandy could see of her was her huge lilac hat with its bunches of cherries around the brim.

'As I recall,' Walter Pickard said slowly, '*traditionally . . .*' he glanced along the row towards Mrs McFarlane, '. . . it was only the menfolk who went in for morris dancing. I don't think many of us in Welford would fancy it!'

There were loud rumbles of agreement. Mandy caught Walter's eye and beamed her thanks.

'Any other comments?' Eileen Davy asked briskly. She allowed a mere couple of seconds before continuing. 'In that case, the committee have no hesitation in voting unanimously in favour. Thank you, Mandy and James.'

James was the first to come down to earth and realise they were meant to leave the platform. He nudged Mandy and pointed.

Mandy returned to her seat in a dreamy haze. She and James had done it! Welford's pets and farm animals would follow the rushcart to church and have their own special service!

Mandy could hardly wait to get home and start planning things. But first there was the rest of the meeting to sit through. And next on the agenda was the question of what should be done with the village pond.

This item had been held over from the last meeting to give everyone a chance to think up some ideas. Mandy hid a grin when Mrs Ponsonby was the first one called to the platform to put her idea forward. Mrs Ponsonby was sure to have thought of something really impressive and probably impossible, Mandy thought mischievously.

Mrs Ponsonby rose majestically and started to make her way slowly and regally to the platform. When she reached the steps, Mr Markham moved towards her, offering his arm. Mrs Ponsonby laid her hand lightly on his arm then, once on the platform, she waved him away as if she was swatting at a fly.

She turned to face her audience, peering happily at them through the lenses of her blue, winged spectacles. 'I know you'll *all* approve of my idea,' she said confidently. 'There's one thing and one thing only that would set our pond off to absolute perfection! And that is . . .' she paused for effect, '. . . a statue of a mermaid. A *bronze* mermaid sitting in the centre of the pond, looking into a mirror made from a mother-of-pearl shell. The mermaid will hold the shell mirror, like this!'

Using both hands, Mrs Ponsonby held her

small clutch-bag a little way in front of her and bowed her head slightly. Mandy thought she looked like a choirboy trying to read a song sheet!

'That's why Mrs Ponsonby didn't object to our idea, James!' whispered Mandy. 'She was too busy rehearsing her little performance.'

Mrs Ponsonby held her pose for a while, waiting in vain for the applause she expected from her audience. Then she looked up and said sorrowfully, 'You're not visualising!'

Tucking her bag firmly under one arm, she said, 'A mermaid is this shape . . .' Her chubby fingers fluttered as she drew a picture in the air. And as her hands moved, so did the large scarlet roses that patterned her silk dress.

All eyes were on her now. Mrs Ponsonby had a captive audience! 'The mermaid is bronze, remember,' she told them. 'And when the sun shines down on her, the bronze will shine and so will the mother-of-pearl mirror that she's holding in her hands. And you'll be able to see the mermaid's face reflected in the mirror!' Mrs Ponsonby's hands fluttered again, Mandy heard someone snort and guessed it was probably Ernie or Walter.

Then Tommy Pickard waved his hands in

the air. 'Please,' he said, 'I've got another question.'

'All right, Tommy. What is your question?' asked Miss Davy.

'How will we be able to see the mermaid's face in the mirror? It's a big pond. We won't even be able to see the mirror!'

'The young 'un has a point there,' said Walter, smiling proudly.

'He has,' agreed Ernie Bell. 'And here's another point. How could we afford something like a bronze statue anyway?'

'I'm grateful to you for raising that question,' Mrs Ponsonby bowed in Ernie's direction. 'I, myself, am willing to pay for the mermaid. And to express your gratitude, I'm sure you wouldn't mind if I had my name on a little plaque on the big tree next to the pond.'

'Your kind offer has been noted, Mrs Ponsonby,' said Miss Davy. 'Now, I think Mrs McFarlane has an idea to put forward?'

Mrs Ponsonby bowed before leaving the platform to walk slowly back to her seat.

Mrs McFarlane didn't bother to go on to the platform. She simply stood up and said loudly, 'I think little fishing gnomes arranged all round the pond would look nice.'

'Thank you, Mrs McFarlane. Are there any more suggestions?'

Flo Maynard suggested a little waterfall fountain. Then Mandy's grandad stood up. 'The only thing our pond needs to make it even more attractive is some pond plants,' he said firmly.

'That's right,' agreed Walter Pickard. 'We should keep it looking natural, not try and pretty it up with fancy bits and bobs.'

'A little wooden bridge would look good,' someone suggested nervously.

'Or a rockery at one end,' said someone else.

'We've heard so many ideas, I think the fairest thing would be for us all to think them over until the next meeting,' said Miss Davy. 'Then we'll take a vote.'

'No decision on what to do with the pond again!' Ernie Bell grumbled on his way out. 'That's the same as happened last time! I would have thought you two could've come up with something that everybody would have wanted to vote for *tonight*!' he added, glaring at James and Mandy. Sitting for such a long time had made poor Ernie grouchy.

'We'll try to think of something for the next meeting, Ernie,' said James.

'Something needs doing before then,' said Walter Pickard. 'It's Saturday tomorrow. How about you and the young miss . . .'

Mandy wasn't listening; she was looking towards the church, imagining the scene of the rushcart and all the animals and their owners.

'I'm sure we could do that, Walter,' said James. 'Couldn't we, Mandy?'

'Yes, of course,' agreed Mandy, trying to work out how many animals there'd be at the special service.

'Shall I come round early in the morning then?' said James.

'Fine,' Mandy said, her mind still elsewhere.

'Come on, Mandy,' Mr Hope ruffled her hair. 'Your mum will be waiting to hear all about the meeting!'

Two

Mandy was up early; by half-past seven she was busy doing her chores in the residential unit. She cleaned out cages and talked to the guinea-pig, the rabbit and the soft, fluffy kitten who'd been kept in overnight. Then she knelt down to talk to Maisy, the young Dalmatian who'd stolen her heart.

Maisy's spots were liver brown; her nose was brown, too, and her beautiful eyes were amber. But Maisy wasn't as lively and alert as she should be for her age; Mandy's parents were keeping her at Animal Ark for a couple of days for observation and some tests.

'You're quite lively this morning, aren't you

girl!' said Mandy, chuckling as Maisy jumped up at the cage door. 'OK, OK, I'll open the door and give you a cuddle.'

At first, Maisy's tail wagged crazily as Mandy petted and talked to her. But after a while the dog seemed to lose all interest; she lay down across Mandy's lap and stared into space.

'All right, back you go,' said Mandy, moving the dog gently from her lap. But Maisy just stood where Mandy had put her. With a sigh Mandy lifted her up and put her back in the cage. 'Never mind, sweetheart,' she said. 'Mum and Dad will soon find out what's wrong with you. Then they can make you better. And Elise will be popping in to see you later today.'

Mandy really liked Elise Knight, Maisy's owner. She was a few years younger than Mrs Hope; small, slim and pretty with shoulder-length hair which was almost the same colour as Maisy's eyes. She'd only recently moved into one of the cottages behind the Fox and Goose. She was a writer and worked from home. Walter Pickard and Ernie Bell lived in the same row of cottages; they were delighted to have such a young and interesting neighbour.

Elise hadn't been at the meeting last night.

I'll tell her all about it, Mandy thought as she made her way to the treatment rooms. *Maybe she'll let Maisy take part in the procession!*

Mandy checked over the treatment rooms, then tidied the racks of pamphlets in Reception. When Simon, Animal Ark's practice nurse, arrived at half-past eight, the whole place was spotless and ready for surgery.

'Good morning, Mandy. How did the meeting go?' he asked.

'Brilliantly!' replied Mandy, and told him all about it.

'It's a great idea, Mandy!' said Simon when she'd finished.

Just then Mandy heard the loud ringing of a bicycle bell. 'Here's James!' she said. 'He's early.' She smiled at Simon and hurried out.

''Morning, Mandy,' said James. 'I've been thinking. There are a few people we ought to go and tell about the procession.'

'They'll know about it soon enough,' laughed Mandy. 'We could put some posters up but I'm sure everybody will be talking about it.'

'The Parker Smythes might not hear about it; they don't come down into the village much,' said James. 'And it would be a shame if Imogen missed out on bringing Barney and Button.'

Mandy nodded at this. She and James were very fond of Imogen Parker Smythe's pretty fawn rabbits.

'Then there's the Spry twins,' James went on. 'They don't get out much. I'm sure they'd love to bring Patch to follow the procession. I thought we could pop in on them on our way back from Walton.'

'On our way back from Walton? When?' asked Mandy.

'I *thought* you weren't really listening last night,' said James. 'Walter Pickard asked if we'd go to the garden centre and take some photos of the ponds they've got there.'

'And we said yes, did we?' laughed Mandy. 'But tell me, James. Why does Walter want the photos?'

'To show everybody what the village pond *could* look like. There are two big ponds at the garden centre, remember! They've both got all sorts of waterlilies and other pond plants growing in them. I agree with Walter and your grandad. Our pond should be kept as natural-looking as possible.'

'Yes, it should,' agreed Mandy. 'We certainly don't want a bronze mermaid. And taking photos of the ponds at the garden centre is a brilliant idea. OK, then, I'll just go and tell Mum where we're going.'

Mandy loved going to the garden centre. She'd been there a few times with her grandad who was a keen gardener. There was an indoor 'Aquaria' section; as well as aquariums with newts and salamanders, there were vivariums housing snakes and other creatures.

And today there were some baby lizards! Mandy and James were fascinated by them, though Mandy noticed that one of them had a swollen eyelid and crouched down to try and get a closer look.

'I'm a bit worried about that little one,' said a voice behind her. Mandy turned round to see Philip Meakin, the owner, standing there.

Mandy smiled at him. She liked the big, bluff man. He was an animal-lover and took good care of the reptiles and amphibians.

'Yes, there's a couple of these tiny fellows I'm not too happy about,' he continued with a worried frown. 'I'll be bringing them to Animal Ark on Monday, Mandy. But what's brought you here, today? Are you after something for your grandad?'

'Not this time,' Mandy replied. 'We'd like to

take some photos of the ponds if that's OK?'
She and James explained about the competition
Welford had entered, and told him about the
suggestions for the village pond.

'Can you imagine how awful a bronze
mermaid or fishing gnomes would look?' said
James. 'If I can get some good photos of the
ponds here, they might help everyone see that
all our pond needs is a few plants!'

'You know, I lived in Welford until I was ten,'
said Philip Meakin. 'Your dad and I were in the
same class at primary school, Mandy! I've got
some happy memories of that pond. I agree
with you, a mermaid or fishing gnomes
wouldn't be the thing at all. Let's see,' he
added, 'the pond's about the size of a tennis
court, right?'

'Near enough,' agreed James.

'With rounded edges, though,' said Mandy.

'Well, perhaps when I bring the lizards to the
surgery, I could find some sample pond plants
to bring as well. A couple of large waterlilies
and some water iris, maybe. I'm sure you'll find
someone willing to help the plants appear in
Welford's pond by chance,' he chuckled. 'Along
with the photos you're going to take, they just
might do the trick.'

'That would be great, Philip. Thank you!' said Mandy.

James took a dozen or so photos, finishing off the film in Walter's camera, so they decided to take it in to the Walton chemist's.

'We can pick the photos up after school on Monday,' said James. 'Maybe Walter will put them on display in the village hall so everyone will have a chance to look at them before the next meeting.'

Mandy smiled. James was getting really enthusiastic about this!

'I think it was terrific of Philip to say he'd bring us some sample plants!' said James, as they cycled back to Welford.

'So was his idea of someone sort of sneaking them into the pond,' laughed Mandy.

'Don't forget we want to see the Spry twins,' said James as they got close to The Riddings, a big old house set back from the road.

'Oh, no! There's Mum's car,' Mandy gasped as they turned into the drive. 'There must be something wrong with Patch!' Patch was the Spry twins' little cat. He was the first pet they'd owned for a long time; the twins were quite old and they tended to panic a bit about him.

'It looks like your mum's just leaving,' said James, as Emily Hope appeared at the front door.

Mandy leaped off her bike and dashed up to her mum.

'It's all right, Mandy,' Mrs Hope said. 'Something frightened poor Patch. He ran into the conservatory and tried to climb that huge prickly cactus they've got in there. I've removed a couple of prickles from his front paw and treated him for shock.'

Mrs Hope glanced quickly behind her then said quietly, 'I think Miss Joan is more shaken up than Patch.'

'We were stopping by anyway, Mrs Hope,' said James. 'To tell Miss Marjorie and Miss Joan about the procession.'

'That's good.' Mrs Hope nodded. 'It will help take Miss Joan's mind off Patch.'

'Shall James and I go in then, Mum?' asked Mandy.

'Yes, I'm sure it will be OK. They're all in the kitchen.'

Going inside The Riddings was like stepping back in time. There were old-fashioned chairs, a huge and ugly coat-stand and an umbrella stand shaped like a buffalo's foot.

'It's not as dreary as it used to be,' said Mandy, looking round. 'They've polished the furniture and taken some of the dark pictures off the walls, and filled the big, old vases with flowers.'

'One thing hasn't changed, though,' said James, as he and Mandy made their way to the back of the house. 'Listen!'

Mandy grinned at the sound of raised voices. The Spry twins were arguing again!

'I tell you, Marjorie, they *weren't* gulls! My eyes are better than yours and I was *there* when they swooped down from the sky. They were much too big for gulls *and* they were white. You don't get pure white gulls round here!'

'Rubbish, Joan. You don't know what you're talking about!'

'I do so!' screeched Miss Joan. 'Besides, Patch isn't scared of gulls and he *was* frightened! So there! That settles it!'

The kitchen door was open, but Mandy tapped loudly on it before she and James went in. 'Hello, Miss Marjorie, Miss Joan,' she said. 'James and I have come to see Patch and to tell you about a very important event.'

'If you've come to tell us about two strange, enormous, white birds, we already know!' said

Miss Joan. 'They frightened poor Patch, flying down low like that. On their way to the river, that's where they were making for.'

'Take no notice of my sister. They weren't strange birds. They were gulls,' said Miss Marjorie. 'I'm the older twin, I should know.'

'That's true. You *are* older. That means your eyesight isn't as good as mine!'

Hiding a smile, Mandy walked past the twins to the window ledge, where Patch lay stretched out in the sunniest spot. 'Who's a poor boy then?' she asked softly. 'Is your paw a bit sore? Let me see. Oh,' she raised her voice slightly, 'I'm sure it will be better in time for you to come to the church on Rushcart Day.'

'Patch come to the church? Whatever are you talking about?' asked Miss Joan, the argument with her twin forgotten for the moment.

Ten minutes later, Mandy and James left the Spry twins arguing still about what sort of birds had frightened Patch.

'At least they both agreed to bring Patch to the procession,' said Mandy.

'Yes,' replied James, shoving his glasses further up the bridge of his nose. 'I wonder what the birds were, though? Miss Joan said they were making for the river.'

'I don't know,' said Mandy. 'You don't want to go and look now, do you? I want my lunch. I'm starving!'

'How about a picnic by the river?' suggested James. 'We could buy some rolls and crisps from the post office.'

'OK,' agreed Mandy. She knew James liked to report sightings of any new birds to the Welford Wildlife Watchers.

Mrs McFarlane, Flo Maynard and Mrs Ponsonby were in the middle of a heated discussion when Mandy and James walked into the shop.

'My nephew is an architect,' Mrs Ponsonby said grandly. 'I've asked him to make a sketch of a mermaid statue.'

'I read somewhere that mermaids are unlucky,' said Mrs McFarlane. 'We don't want anything that might bring bad luck to Welford. Besides, don't you think fishing gnomes would look much friendlier?'

'A waterfall fountain would look friendly *and* pretty!' said Flo Maynard. 'I recall . . .'

'Cripes!' James muttered, shaking his head. 'Everyone seems to be arguing today.'

Mandy nodded, picking up some cheese rolls and taking them to the counter. She was just deciding what flavour crisps to buy when Mrs Markham came into the shop.

'I've just had a really frightening experience!' she said. 'I was walking Bunty along the riverbank when all of a sudden two swans swooped down and landed just in front of us. Well, I know two swans live on our river so I wasn't too bothered at first, even though they'd made me jump! But then two more swans came and started attacking the first ones! They were all hissing and pecking and flapping their wings. There were feathers flying everywhere! I didn't dare stop to help! I was scared Bunty might get in their way and get hurt! And we're going away for the weekend. Robert's waiting to leave. I—'

'Mrs Markham,' Mandy interrupted. 'Were they all big swans? There are some baby swans on the river as well.'

'There are *five* cygnets,' added James. 'This year's the first time the swans have nested here.'

'They *might* have been on the water,' said Mrs Markham. 'I didn't stop to look. The four who were fighting were enormous! I think they'd already had one scrap. I heard a lot of honking when I was walking down the footpath. But I didn't see anything until they all landed in front of me like that. Really,' she shuddered, 'they looked set to half kill each other. I've never seen . . .'

James didn't wait to hear any more; he was out of the shop like a streak of lightning. Mandy threw some money on the counter and ran after him.

'Manners today!' she heard Mrs Ponsonby say. 'I don't know what . . .'

There was a footpath by the side of the post office. Cycling along it wasn't allowed, but James and Mandy ignored the rules and pedalled madly towards the river. This was an emergency!

Three

'It must have been swans that Miss Joan saw,' panted Mandy. 'She said they were enormous birds. And that they were pure white. Maybe our swans were trying to see them off, to protect their family!'

'Which way, Mandy?' said James, peering up and down the length of the river. 'Which way shall we go?'

'They're usually up that way, aren't they?' Mandy pointed to the right. 'And look, James! Isn't that Brandon along there?'

James looked towards the water's edge. 'Yes, you're right. Come on, Mandy. Maybe he's found something.'

Brandon Gill was in Mandy's class at school.
He lived at Greystones Farm, which was further
up the river at the end of a long track. 'Hello,'
he said, looking up as James and Mandy skidded
to a halt on the riverbank above him. 'What's
up?'

'Mrs Markham saw some swans fighting,'
explained Mandy. 'We're worried in case any
are badly hurt. And we want to see if their babies
are safe. When we saw you down here, we
thought you'd seen something.'

'Two swans passed a while ago. Going that
way.' He pointed down river. 'I didn't take that
much notice of them. But now I think about it,'
Brandon glanced worriedly at them, 'I didn't
see the cygnets. Just the two big ones.'

'It might have been the newcomers you saw,'
James said hopefully.

'It might not,' said Mandy. 'And even if it was,
we've got to try and find the other swans and
make sure they're all OK. The newcomers might
have attacked the cygnets, James! *That* could
have been what the big fight was about!'

'What shall we do now?' asked James. 'Go on,
or go back the other way?'

'I came on my bike,' said Brandon. 'You two
go back, the way the swans went, and I'll carry

on up river. If I find anything I'll come and fetch you.'

James and Mandy cycled for some time without seeing anything. 'Even the ducks aren't around,' sighed Mandy. But a few metres further on a movement ahead caught Mandy's eye. 'Look, James!' she said, braking. 'On the other side, just where the river bends . . . coming this way . . .' She held up a hand to shade her eyes.

'Two swans, no cygnets,' James said glumly.

'Well, at least we can try and see if *they're* all right,' Mandy said huskily. 'I'll throw a bit of our rolls in when they get closer. They seem to be moving normally, don't they?'

James stared across at them and nodded. 'I think so. Except they're very close together and one's got its head turned away and its neck's bent. We can't really see if they're injured or not. Throw the bread in now, Mandy.'

But the swans ignored it, swimming slowly on.

'What shall we do now?' asked James. 'Is it worth going on?'

'If those two are the parent swans maybe they've hidden the cygnets somewhere,' Mandy said hopefully.

'Or maybe the cygnets swam off on their own

because they were hurt or frightened,' said James. 'If only we knew exactly *where* Mrs Markham saw the fight. I wouldn't have thought she'd have come this far. She – '

James broke off and stared at Mandy. '*That's* what we'll do,' he said. 'Go and ask Mrs Markham where she saw the swans fighting!'

'We can't!' said Mandy. 'Remember what she said in the post office, James? She said they were going away for the weekend. Mr Markham was ready to leave, so they'll be gone by now!'

'Well, somebody else might have seen the fight or an injured swan and phoned Animal Ark!' said James. 'Come on, Mandy, let's find out.'

Mandy's parents and Simon were eating lunch in the garden. 'Help yourself to some soup and rolls, you two,' said Mrs Hope. 'You haven't been at The Riddings all this time, have you?' she added.

Mandy shook her head. 'We've been down by the river. Has anyone phoned to report an injured swan, Mum?'

'No, love. Why?'

'You know the birds that frightened Patch?

Well, we think they were swans.' Mandy took a deep breath and went on to tell them about the fight Mrs Markham had seen. 'We saw two adult swans but we weren't really sure if they were all right,' Mandy finished breathlessly. 'And we don't know if they were the parent swans or the new ones.'

'We're really worried about the cygnets, Mrs Hope,' said James. 'What if the newcomers attacked them? They could be badly hurt!'

'Or the parents might have been hurt,' said Mandy.

'The newcomers wouldn't have gone for the young swans,' said Simon. 'But you're right, Mandy. The parent swans might have been hurt. Because they're rearing a family, they'll have made a heck of an effort to try and see the newcomers off.'

'You'd better make another search, Mandy,' said Mr Hope. 'I can't come with you, I'm on call. But there's still a couple of hours till afternoon surgery,' he looked inquiringly at his wife.

'I want to run a few more tests on Maisy,' said Mrs Hope. 'You could go, Simon. There's no dressings or medications to do and, apart from Maisy, all the residents have been collected.'

Simon was already on his feet. 'I'll go and get an emergency pack, just in case we need it,' he said. 'Best take some bread as well.'

Mandy was the first to spot the swan family when they reached the river. 'Look!' she said excitedly, grabbing James and Simon who were looking the other way. 'Over there, on the far side.'

'Mum, Dad and all five babies!' said James. Then he and Mandy dashed forward and slid down the banking.

'They seem to be all right, don't they!' said James. He pushed his glasses further back on his

nose and stared across the water, smiling happily.

'Yes, they do!' agreed Mandy. She turned her head to look up at Simon. 'What do you think, Simon? Are they OK?'

'I'd like a closer look,' he said. 'Throw them some bread, Mandy. Hopefully it'll persuade them to come over to this side.'

It did. And as they swam closer Mandy could see bald patches on the adults' necks. 'They've lost a lot of feathers,' she said.

Simon was at the water's edge now and he nodded. 'I don't think there are any actual wounds though,' he said.

'But look!' James pointed. 'That one's got one leg bent up, Simon. It must be hurt!'

'It's OK,' said Simon. 'Most swans swim and rest on the water, with one leg on their back.'

'Three of the cygnets are swimming like that, too,' said Mandy. 'Copying their mum.'

'It's their *dad*,' said Simon. 'See the knob at the base of its beak? It's more prominent on the male swans.'

'Oh, yes,' said Mandy. 'I hadn't noticed that. Oh, I'm so glad they're all right,' she added. 'Apart from a few missing feathers, the fight doesn't seem to have harmed or upset them at all, does it?'

'No,' said Simon. 'I'm sure they wouldn't come so close to us if it had.'

'What about the other swans, though?' said James. 'We don't know for sure which two it was we saw earlier. They didn't come close enough for us to see if there were any feathers missing.'

'Let's walk on for a while and see if they're around,' suggested Mandy.

'Simon, why do you think the other swans decided to come here?' asked James.

'There's been quite a large increase in the swan population over the last two or three years,' said Simon. 'They were talking about it on *Wildlife Ways* last week. That means there'll be more swans looking for new areas to inhabit.'

'So the new ones might make their home here?' said Mandy. 'If the others will let them.'

'They probably will in the end,' said Simon. 'As long as the new ones don't try and get too close.'

They walked on for a while but there was no sign of the other swans so they turned round and made their way back.

'Do you feel like playing tennis this evening, Mandy?' asked James. 'We could work out the wording for the posters afterwards, then make a start on them tomorrow.'

'All right,' agreed Mandy. 'I'll meet you by the courts about six-thirty. Surgery should be finished by then.' Saturday afternoon surgery was often a busy one and Mandy liked to help out.

When Simon and Mandy arrived back at Animal Ark, Emily Hope was just taking Maisy back into the residential unit. Mandy thought her mum looked a bit worried. 'Have you done the tests, Mum?' she asked.

'Yes I have, Mandy. But no questions, please, love. I need to talk things over with Dad first.'

'OK,' said Mandy. She didn't like having to wait but she knew her parents would tell her what was wrong with Maisy as soon as they could.

Afternoon surgery was very busy. It was quarter to seven by the time Mandy cycled off to meet James at the tennis courts.

'I wish you'd been there, James,' she said. 'It was more like a zoo than the usual sort of surgery. There was a parrot, a canary and a budgie, a racing pigeon; a snake with blisters, a twenty-year-old tortoise with an eye infection, three yowling Siamese cats and a rabbit with hiccups!'

James laughed; he loved hearing about the animals who went to Animal Ark. 'That's just what the procession will be like,' he said. 'Look,' he added, 'here's Elise Knight coming over to us. I wonder if she's heard about the procession? I'm sure she'd like to bring Maisy.'

'Hello, Mandy,' said Elise. Then she turned to James. 'I've just had a very tough game with your mother,' she told him. 'It helped to take my mind off things for a while. I'm really missing Maisy. She's often quite naughty and won't do as she's told, but I love her all the same.'

'She's a lovely dog,' said Mandy. 'It's no wonder you're missing her. Oh, look, James, there's a court free. We could get it before anyone else does.' She rushed away with a wave at Elise.

'Why the rush?' James asked as he caught up with Mandy. 'I thought you liked Elise. And we didn't tell her about the procession.'

'I do like her, James. She's terrific. But I didn't want her to ask me any questions about Maisy.'

'Why? Your parents haven't found something seriously wrong with her, have they?'

'I don't know,' replied Mandy. 'Mum seemed a bit worried when I asked about the tests she did this afternoon. She wouldn't tell me anything though. She said she needed to discuss something with Dad. And Dad's having an old friend round for supper. So I won't know anything until tomorrow!'

Four

'Brandon phoned to ask if he could borrow my homework notes so I said I'd take them round,' Mandy told her mum. 'And there's a plate of salad in the fridge for you. I've had mine.'

It was the first time Mandy had seen either of her parents since the previous night. Adam Hope had left very early to go to an agricultural show where he was duty vet, and Emily Hope had just returned from delivering a calf at one of the farms.

'Any excuse to see the pigs!' laughed Mrs Hope.

'And to check on the swans,' said Mandy. 'I'm meeting James by the post office and we're going the river way. Is it OK if I take some bread?'

'Yes, you can take what's left of the open loaf,' her mother nodded. 'I've asked Elise Knight to come round this afternoon, Mandy. Maisy can go home but I need to have a long talk with Elise first.'

'You know what's wrong with Maisy, don't you, Mum? Can you tell me about it now? Is it serious?' asked Mandy anxiously.

'Well, it's certainly a difficult problem, love. I'm afraid Maisy's deaf. Not totally deaf,' she added. 'Both Dad and I are sure she's got a certain amount of hearing in one ear.'

Mandy's heart sank. 'So is that why Maisy isn't very lively sometimes? Because she can't hear what's being said to her? Oh, Mum, that's terrible! But isn't there an operation she can have, to make her hear better?'

'I'm afraid there isn't, love. That's the problem. It will be very hard for Maisy to lead a normal, active life. A dog like Maisy needs a lot of exercise. Long walks on the lead aren't really enough. She needs to be able to run free at times as well. Elise told me she had a huge garden where she used to live. Here, she has hardly any at all.'

'But . . .' Mandy looked puzzled. 'I don't understand, Mum. Being deaf won't stop Maisy from running round, will it? Oh!' she gasped. 'I think I see what you mean! Elise will have to take Maisy somewhere like the field near the tennis courts and let her off the lead for a run. But Maisy won't be able to hear when Elise calls her back. Is that it, Mum?'

Mrs Hope nodded. 'That's the sort of thing I need to talk to Elise about, Mandy,' she said. 'It's possible Maisy might respond to hand signals and possibly to a high-pitched whistle.'

'You mean one of those whistles *we* can't hear but animals can?'

Mrs Hope nodded again. 'Yes, I think Maisy might hear a slight sound from that sort of whistle. Training her to recognise it and react to it would be very hard work, though, and very time-consuming.'

'Well, we break up next week so I could help sometimes,' said Mandy. 'And I'm sure James would help, too. Is there anything we could read about training a deaf dog, Mum?'

'I've seen an article in one of the magazines,' said Mrs Hope. 'But we'll see how Elise feels about it all, first. Now you'd better go, Mandy. James will be wondering where you've got to.'

'Can I go and give Maisy a cuddle first?' asked Mandy. 'She'll be able to *feel* that even if she can't hear what I'm saying.'

'All right,' replied Mrs Hope, giving Mandy a quick hug. 'I'll come with you.'

They went through to the residential unit and Mandy knelt down to open Maisy's cage door. Maisy looked at Mandy and wagged her tail. 'Here, girl!' said Mandy, slapping her hands against her knees. 'Come on, Maisy. Come on.'

Maisy bounded forward and put her front legs up on Mandy's shoulders.

'There, Mum,' said Mandy, rubbing her face against Maisy's chest and blinking hard. 'Maisy came to me when I slapped my hands on my knees. That's one hand signal she'll learn easily enough.'

'But only if she's facing the right way, love,' Mrs Hope said gently. 'Now, come on. Finish your cuddle and get off to meet James.'

'Oh, poor Maisy!' said James, when Mandy told him what was wrong.

'I don't know what will happen to her if Elise doesn't think she can cope,' Mandy said miserably. 'I didn't dare ask Mum that!'

James dropped his bike down in the grass,

moved to the water's edge and started jumping
from rock to rock. Then he rejoined Mandy and
said firmly, 'Elise really loves Maisy. She'll
manage. And your parents will give her plenty
of advice. They're terrific at helping with
problems. And maybe we could help, too.
Even though I haven't been very successful in
training Blackie,' he added with a smile.

Mandy smiled back. James really was a good
friend! 'I've already told Mum that we'd help,'
she said softly.

James picked his bike up and they walked on
in silence for a while. It was a sunny afternoon
but there was a slight breeze. If she listened
hard, Mandy could hear the water murmuring
its way over the pebbles.

Before long, two swans appeared, swimming
towards them. 'Look, James!' said Mandy,
tugging his arm. 'They haven't got any cygnets
with them.'

'They must be the newcomers,' said James.
'Maybe they've decided to stay. Do you think
they'll come close to us this time, Mandy?'

'Yes! Look, James, they've changed course a
bit. I'm sure they're coming across to us. Yes,
they are! They are, James! I brought some bread
in case we saw them! It's in my saddlebox.'

Mandy flicked the box open and reached for the bread.

'I brought some, too,' said James, opening the small knapsack that he'd strapped to his bike's handlebars. They laid their bikes down and, carefully and slowly so as not to alarm the swans, made their way down the banking to the water's edge.

'Start tearing the bread into small pieces and throw it in!' Mandy whispered urgently. 'Quick, James, they're almost here!'

'You take the one on the left, I'll take the other one,' said James. 'Then they won't fight over the same piece. Wow! Mandy! Did you see that? My swan almost caught a piece!'

Mandy chuckled. The swan she was throwing bread to was treading water; coming closer and closer to her. It was now only half a metre away.

Then Mandy gave a loud gasp as the swan suddenly stretched its long neck out and snatched what remained of the slice of bread right out of her fingers. When it had gobbled it down, it made a strange hissing noise.

'I think it's asking for another piece,' whispered James. 'Change places with me and let me do it, Mandy.' James tore the crust from a

slice of bread and held it out to the swan, who took it so quickly that James's fingers nearly disappeared inside its beak.

Mandy held some bread out to the other swan. It wouldn't take it from her fingers so she dropped it into the water. 'I wonder if they're male or female?' she said. 'Simon told us the knob on a male swan's beak is more prominent than the one on the female's. But . . .' Mandy looked from one swan to the other.

James nodded. 'Both knobs are the same size, so we can't tell. Cripes! Did you see that?' he added. 'It just snatched a whole slice right out of my hand.'

'Look, this one's got a bald patch on its chest,' Mandy pointed out.

'And greedy guts here has got bald patches on the top of its head,' said James. 'That proves it for sure. These swans must be the ones the parent swans had a fight with.'

The greedy swan hissed again. 'You've eaten it all,' replied Mandy. 'We'll ask Brandon's mum if she's got any bread to spare and give it to you on our way back.'

'Ssss!' said the swan. Then it rose up in the water, spreading its huge white wings.

'It's no good your getting bad-tempered!'

Mandy said sternly. 'We haven't got any more and that's that!'

'Ssss!' said the swan, sinking back into the water.

'Whew!' said James, letting out his breath in a huge sigh of relief. 'I really thought it was getting angry then, Mandy. Swans can be dangerous when they're annoyed!'

'Don't let them know you're frightened,' said Mandy. 'That's the trick.'

'Were you frightened?' asked James, as they made their way back up the banking.

'Let's say I was a little bit worried,' Mandy grinned as she picked her bike up. 'Still, the poor things could have flown miles looking for a place to settle. They're probably starving hungry.'

'What *do* swans eat?' asked James. 'Apart from bread, I mean!'

But Mandy wasn't sure. 'Pondweed and water insects, I suppose,' she said. 'We'll have to ask Simon.'

When Mandy and James arrived at Greystones Farm, they heard Brandon before they saw him. 'Yip, yip! Yip, yip, yip!' He was calling to the pigs.

They propped their bikes against a wall and

dashed up to the top field. They loved watching the Gills' plump, squealing pigs charging to the food troughs.

Brandon's young brother and sisters were feeding the pigs, too. Mandy smiled as the twins, Christopher and Lola, bustled around. 'Ip-yip-ip, pigs!' they chorused in unison.

'It's *yip*, yip!' Angela, Brandon's sister, corrected them. Then she caught sight of James and Mandy. 'James!' she called, hurrying across the field, her brown ponytail bobbing madly. 'Have you come to see Harry? He's had some more babies!' Harry was Angela's gerbil. And even though Harry had produced several litters of babies, Angela refused to change Harry's name to Harriet!

'I think Angela's your number one fan, James,' teased Mandy. James blushed.

'The little 'uns have started to take an interest in the pigs,' Angela told them, sounding very grown-up. 'I'd rather have gerbils myself. Are you coming to see them then, James? You can come, too, Mandy,' she added.

Mandy smiled down at the little girl. 'Thank you, Angela, we'd love to see them. Is your mum indoors? James and I want to ask her something.'

'I'll be finished in a few minutes!' Brandon

called. 'You go on in with Angela.'

Harry and her new litter were duly admired. Then Mrs Gill told James and Mandy she'd be bringing Angela, the twins, Harry the gerbil and Maggie the farm dog to the procession.

'That's terrific, Mrs Gill!' said James. And then Mandy asked her shyly if she had any bread to spare.

'There's always plenty of bread on a pig farm,' laughed Brandon, who'd just joined them. 'The pigs like a slice or two in with their morning feed. Does that mean you've found the swans? Are they OK?'

'I think the two you saw yesterday were the newcomers, Brandon,' said James. 'We saw them shortly after we'd left you but they wouldn't come anywhere near us. Then later on we found the other swans *and* their cygnets.'

'The parents had a few feathers missing,' said Mandy. 'But nothing worse. We've not seen *them* today. But we've seen the new ones.'

'That's grand,' said Brandon. 'Are the new ones friendlier today, then?'

'I don't know about friendly,' said James. 'They're pretty greedy. At least, one of them is. It snatched the bread from us, then hissed when it was all gone!'

'We said we'd take her some more bread if we could,' said Mandy and James looked surprised. 'I *know* we don't know if they're male or female,' said Mandy, 'but I don't like calling anything "it". Besides, I think they are female.'

'Pens,' said Brandon.

'Pens! Why's Mandy feeding pens with bread? That's silly!' lisped little Lola.

Brandon chuckled and picked her up. 'That's what a girl swan is called, Lola. A pen. A boy swan is called a cob!'

'That's silly, too!' giggled Lola.

'It might be silly but it's the right thing to call them, Lola. A girl is a pen and a boy is a cob. OK?'

'OK, Brandon.' Lola nodded solemnly then wriggled away from him. She went over to her twin. 'Let's go back to the pigs, Christopher,' she said. 'And 'member, the girl ones are pens and the boy ones are cobs.'

'Now see what you've done, Brandon!' laughed Mrs Gill, handing Mandy a carrier bag with some bread in it.

'Aye,' agreed Brandon. 'I seem to have muddled them up good and proper!'

Brandon went outside with them and Mandy gave him the homework notes he needed. Then, still smiling about the twins, she and James cycled out of the farmyard and back towards the river.

They'd only gone a few metres when they both braked to a sudden stop and stared ahead in disbelief. The two swans were coming towards them. Not swimming on the water but marching, side by side on enormous feet, along the riverbank!

'Do you think they came looking for us?' gasped Mandy.

James pushed his glasses further back on his nose. 'I don't know,' he replied. 'But I hope they know we're friends. Now that they've seen us they're moving faster!'

'I'm glad we've got something to give them,' said Mandy, busily tearing the bread into small chunks and passing some to James.

As they got closer, the swans turned their heads and looked at each other. Mandy thought it looked as if they were making up their minds what to do next!

She and James watched as the swans moved apart. 'One's coming to you and the other's coming to me,' Mandy said quietly.

'Cripes!' murmured James. 'Do you think we're doing the right thing, just standing here?

They're coming right up close, Mandy!'

Mandy nodded and held her breath. Soon the swans were less than an arm's length away. 'We'd better make sure we don't accidentally move our front wheels,' she said. Then she smiled as the swan who'd chosen her solemnly rested its long neck on her bicycle handlebars.

'Well, you are a brave girl, aren't you!' Keeping one hand on the handlebars, Mandy reached into the carrier bag and pulled out a chunk of bread. The swan took it gently; then waited patiently for Mandy to pass another piece.

The swan who'd gone to James was well-behaved, too. No hissing, grabbing or spreading of wings this time!

When the bread was all gone the swans moved away. Mandy and James walked on for a metre or so, then the swans both turned at exactly the same moment and made their way down the banking to sit side by side at the water's edge.

'Whew! That was quite an experience!' said James. 'I'll have to write it up for the next meeting of the Welford Wildlife Watchers.'

'It was brilliant!' said Mandy. 'They seem to be settling in nicely. I think they *have* decided to stay.'

'They're tucking their heads under their wings now,' said James. 'Sleeping off their meal.'

The church bells ringing for early evening service reminded them of the time. 'I haven't done my homework yet!' said James.

'And I want to make a start on the posters,' said Mandy. 'I thought we could ask Mrs McFarlane to put one up in the shop. That's if she's forgiven us for dashing out like that yesterday!'

'I'll do the one to go on the board outside the village hall,' said James as they cycled on. 'I'll put it up tonight when I take Blackie for his walk.'

James lived at the other end of the village so they split up at the crossroads.

As Mandy turned on to the track behind the Fox and Goose she saw Elise Knight walking towards her cottage. Elise was wiping her eyes with a tissue. She was alone; Maisy wasn't with her!

Five

'Hello, Mandy!' said Elise. 'I've just come from Animal Ark.'

Straddling her bike, Mandy nodded and looked down at the ground. She didn't know what to say! Why hadn't Elise brought Maisy home? Surely she hadn't decided to give up on her?

Elise sniffed and dabbed her eyes again. 'I'm just being silly,' she said. 'But I'm so relieved there isn't anything seriously wrong with Maisy.'

Mandy's head shot up. It didn't sound as if Elise had given up!

Elise went on quickly. 'Oh, I know deafness is really serious, Mandy. But I *can* do something about it. I mean, I know she'll always be deaf, you mum explained that to me. She told me she'd explained to you as well. She was so kind and understanding.'

Mandy smiled and nodded. Her mum was the best!

'She's going to find me some books on training dogs,' said Elise. 'And I'll have to work out which hand signals I can use for Maisy and—'

'But Elise!' Mandy couldn't keep quiet any longer. 'Elise, why isn't Maisy with you? I thought Mum said she could go home.'

'It seemed such a shame to unsettle her by bringing her home then taking her back tomorrow for her operation,' said Elise.

'Operation?' Feeling puzzled, Mandy shook her head.

'Yes. Your mum said if Maisy were to have puppies, they might be deaf, too. They could even be totally deaf! I wouldn't want that, Mandy. So Maisy's having an operation to make sure she won't have any pups.'

'Oh, Elise!' Mandy let out a sigh. 'When I saw you without Maisy I thought . . . Well, I didn't know what to think! Mum said training Maisy would take up a lot of time, and—'

'And you thought I might have decided *I*

didn't have time,' guessed Elise. She smiled at Mandy. 'I'm lucky, Mandy. Working from home means I can organise my hours around training and helping Maisy. Giving her the extra attention she'll need. It'll be hard work but I'll manage. She's not going to be miserable just because she can't hear properly. I'll see to that!'

'James and I could help you if you like, Elise,' Mandy offered eagerly. 'And I'm sure Mum won't mind if you bring Maisy to Animal Ark's garden sometimes. There's more room for training sessions there than in your garden.'

'That would be great! Thank you, Mandy. Oh, here's Mr Pickard coming back from his bell-ringing.' Elise waved to her neighbour.

Mandy turned to wave, too. 'I'll be round after school tomorrow with your photos, Walter!' she called before she cycled off.

Walter was delighted with the photos when Mandy took them round as she'd promised. 'I'll go along to the village hall straight away and put them on the notice-board,' he said.

'It's pouring down, Walter!' You can't go out in this!' protested Mandy.

Walter snorted. 'What's a bit of rain, young miss? Besides, there's a WI meeting tonight. I

want these photos on view for then.' He winked
at Mandy. 'When certain people see how good
our pond could look with plants and suchlike,
they'll soon change their minds about having
fancy bits and bobs like statues and fishing
gnomes and fountains!'

'Well, the Hopes and the Hunters and Ernie
Bell are all with you, Walter!' said Mandy. 'And,
knowing Gran, she'll manage to drum up
support from most of the WI! There's someone
else on our side, too,' she added. 'When James
and I went to the garden centre to take these
photos, Philip Meakin said he might bring a few
sample pond plants with him when he brings
his lizards to Animal Ark. He said he was sure
there'd be someone willing to make the plants
appear by chance in our pond!'

Walter gave a deep chuckle. 'You let me know
if he brings some plants,' he said. 'I'll see to
putting them in the pond. The sooner the
better. I reckon the competition judges will be
starting to make spot checks any time now.
They're bound to look at the pond. Welford's
the only village with a pond on the green out
of all the villages taking part.'

'Right, I'll let you know, Walter,' promised
Mandy as she went out.

As she was passing Elise Knight's cottage, Elise opened an upstairs window and called, 'Mandy! I've just phoned Animal Ark. Maisy's come round from her operation and I should be able to fetch her in the morning!'

'That's great!' shouted Mandy, then she hurried on.

'The competition's really got people going,' said Emily Hope when Mandy told her about Walter's plan for the photographs. 'Philip Meakin brought some pond plants when he came to morning surgery. He said you knew about them, Mandy. And everyone mentioned the procession and the service for the animals.'

'Except Mrs Parker Smythe,' said Mr Hope, coming into the kitchen. 'She's getting as bad as Mrs Ponsonby! She came to see if I could recommend a safe make of paint for the inside of Button and Barney's hutch. She wants to paint it pale blue and pink because they've got important guests coming to stay with them. I nearly asked her if the guests would be sleeping in the rabbits' hutch! Blue and pink paint, I ask you!'

'There is a special paint for the inside of hutches, though, isn't there?' said Mandy thoughtfully. 'But it's green. I've seen it at the pet shop. I could phone Mrs Parker Smythe and tell her about it. And ask about Imogen coming to the procession at the same time.'

'Good idea,' laughed Mrs Hope. 'As long as you're *polite* about it,' she warned her daughter firmly.

Mandy tried on and off for the rest of the week to speak to Mrs Parker Smythe, but the phone was always engaged.

'She's probably phoning someone to complain about the weather!' James said with a grin, when Mandy mentioned it to him. 'It's not stopped raining all week and I bet she wants to arrange tennis parties for their important guests. She told Mum that they'd spent a fortune on having their tennis court resurfaced especially for them!'

'Well, I'm not giving up!' said Mandy. 'It's Saturday tomorrow, so I can try phoning during the day.'

But Saturday morning surgery was hectic. Mr Hope had gone to a meeting in York so Mandy was very busy helping out wherever she could. A violent thunderstorm didn't help matters; most of the patients at Animal Ark needed a lot of calming down.

After lunch, Emily Hope was called out to

Mrs Forsyth's riding stables. Two of her horses had panicked during the storm. They'd tried to kick their way out of their stable, and had injured themselves quite badly.

'Are you coming with me, Mandy?' asked Mrs Hope.

'No, I'll stay here,' said Mandy. 'James has gone to Sheffield with his parents but he said he'd come round when he got back. Besides, I want to try phoning Beacon House again.'

'You don't give up, do you?' said Mrs Hope, smiling as she hurried out.

Mandy was just about to pick up the phone when there was a knock on the kitchen door. It was Jean Knox, Animal Ark's receptionist.

'Mandy, could you possibly man the surgery phone for a little while?' she asked. 'Simon's busy removing a cyst from a dog's chest, so he can't do it. And I can't remember closing my front door when I came out after lunch. I tried phoning my neighbour but she isn't in.'

Mandy followed Jean through to the reception area and smiled when Jean started hunting for her car keys. 'You're using your bike today, Jean. You told me this morning your car had gone in for servicing!' Jean really was the most forgetful person!

'Oh, silly me!' sighed Jean. 'I'll try not to be long,' she added as she hurried out.

Mandy checked to make sure there was a pen handy in case she needed to write an appointment down. Jean sometimes went off with a pen tucked behind each ear! Before long, the phone rang.

'Welford 703267,' said Mandy. 'Animal Ark. Can I help you?'

'Is that Mandy? No, no, you can't help. I need one of your parents. No, I need *both* of your parents at Beacon House now! *Right* now! Oh, why should something like this happen to me!'

'Mrs Parker Smythe,' Mandy interrupted her firmly. 'Is there something wrong with one of the rabbits?'

'Rabbits? What are you talking about? It's the swimming-pool, my beautiful pool. It's . . . it's enormous!'

'Yes, I *know* your swimming-pool is big,' said Mandy. 'But Mrs Parker Smythe, why have you phoned Animal Ark?'

'Why! Why!' Mrs Parker Smythe replied hysterically. 'So someone can come and get it out.' My house guests are due any time. What will they think when they see that great big thing swimming in my beautiful pool? This is—'

'Mrs Parker Smythe!' Mandy interrupted urgently '*What* is swimming in your pool?'

'A swan! An enormous, dangerous-looking swan! It's *swimming* in my beautiful pool. Are you sending your parents to Beacon House? You do realise this is an emergency! My house guests—'

'Someone will be there as soon as possible!' said Mandy, putting the receiver down and cutting Mrs Parker Smythe off in mid-flow. She quickly punched out the number of her mum's mobile phone. There was no reply.

Mandy moved quickly to the filing cabinet where the patients' addresses and phone numbers where kept. She found Mrs Forsyth's phone number and hurried back to the phone. But there was no reply from the riding stables, either.

What was she going to do now?

Six

'Simon!' said Mandy. 'It'll have to be Simon!'

She hurried into the recovery room where Simon was bending over an Old English sheepdog. 'I need to keep an eye on the poor old fellow,' he said. 'He reacted badly to the anaesthetic.'

'Oh, no!' sighed Mandy.

'He'll be OK,' said Simon. 'I've just got to watch he doesn't choke when he's sick.'

'That's the problem!' said Mandy. 'I *was* hoping you'd be able to go to the Parker Smythes. I can't get hold of Mum. She's up at the riding stables. But I've phoned and there's no reply.'

'Can't the Parker Smythes bring the rabbit here?' asked Simon.

'It's not Button or Barney, Simon. A *swan*'s landed in their swimming-pool! It must have flown in through the window.'

'Is the swan hurt, Mandy?' Simon asked quickly. 'Is it cut?'

'Oh, Simon! I didn't ask!' gasped Mandy. 'It was ages before Mrs Parker Smythe got round to tell me why she'd phoned. And when she did—'

'OK, I understand,' said Simon. He shook his head. 'There's no way I can leave Silas. You'll have to go, Mandy. We'll ask Jean to keep trying to get hold of your mum.'

'Jean's not here, but she should be back soon!' said Mandy. 'What shall I take with me, Simon? What will I need to do?'

'OK,' Simon said calmly. 'It sounded as if the swan was conscious, did it?'

Mandy nodded. 'Mrs Parker Smythe said it was swimming!'

'Right. Well, first you'll have to get it out of the pool. You'll need to take some glucose solution and a syringe and dribble some glucose solution from the syringe into its mouth.'

'OK. How do I persuade it to open its mouth though?'

'One hand over its bill, thumb one side, fingers the other . . .' Simon demonstrated with his hand.

Mandy nodded. 'And sort of ease the top bit and bottom bit apart. Then I dribble the glucose solution in?'

Simon nodded. 'Try and do it as soon as you can, Mandy. Swans can go into shock very quickly. They've been known to die after just half an hour's stress. The glucose should help to prevent that. I just hope the swan is able to swallow,' he added. 'Still, with any luck, we'll have managed to contact your mum and she'll be with you by then.'

'What if she isn't? And what if the swan *can't* swallow?' asked Mandy.

'Get Mr or Mrs Parker Smythe to bring you here straight away. I'll have to use a special syringe with a tube on the end and insert the tube into the swan's throat.'

'What's the best way of lifting a swan if I have to get it out to a car?' asked Mandy, urgently. She was anxious to get going but she knew she'd have to know how to deal with everything first.

Simon demonstrated with his hands again. 'Take its head in one hand, OK? And put your other arm round its body. Right over its wings,

Mandy. Be careful not to miss them or you'll have a right struggle *and* you might get hurt.'

'Right.' Mandy nodded and started to move away. 'I'll get the glucose and syringe,' she said.

'Hang on one more second, Mandy!' Simon drew her back. 'This is *very* important. If the wings are cut and bleeding, or if you think they're damaged in any way, wrap something like a towel around the swan's body *before* you pick it up. It will help keep the wings in place and help prevent any dust or dirt getting into the wounds.'

'Right.' Mandy took what she needed from the medicine cabinet, then whirled round and hurried out of the recovery room, muttering Simon's instructions to herself so she wouldn't forget them.

'Mandy? Is something wrong?' Jean Knox had just returned and was walking towards the reception desk.

Mandy quickly told Jean what had happened. 'Simon can't leave the dog and I can't get hold of Mum,' she ended breathlessly.

Jean might be very forgetful and vague at times, but she was brilliant in an emergency. 'Give me that, Mandy,' she said, pointing to the glucose and syringe. 'I'll put it in a carrier bag while you fetch your bike.'

Then she followed Mandy outside and said, 'Here, put the carrier bag over your handlebars. I'll keep phoning until I reach your mum, Mandy.'

'Thanks, Jean.' Mandy was already riding away. 'If Mum doesn't arrive I'll get the swan back somehow,' she called. 'And if James comes, tell him to get to Beacon House as quickly as he can!'

As Mandy cycled past the green, she was vaguely aware of a small knot of people round the village pond and of someone calling her name. But she took no notice. She could only think about getting to the swan!

The long slope up to Beacon House seemed longer and steeper than ever. Mandy's breath came in painful gulps. She was pushing herself to the limit as she forced her legs and feet to turn . . . turn . . . turn the pedals.

Then the hill began to flatten out; she was nearly there! *Please let the gates be open*! Mandy wished silently as she cycled past the high hawthorn hedge that hid the Parker Smythes' ground from view.

They were! Mandy turned in and pedalled

madly down the long drive; past the small wood, past the helicopter pad and towards the big white house . . .

Then round the side of the house and past the giant conservatory, which was the link to the swimming-pool room.

. She could hear voices now: Mrs Parker Smythe's screechy and hysterical; Mr Parker Smythe's deep but despairing; Imogen's high and pleading. Mandy's breath was coming in sobs as she rode past the plate glass windows that formed one side of the pool room. The windows were frosted, so she couldn't see in. But at least she could see that none of them was broken!

Then Mandy nipped round the corner to the front of the glass building. She grabbed the carrier bag and was off her bike in a flash. The huge French doors leading into the pool were wide open! Mandy ran inside.

The poolside was a dazzling white, the water deep blue. The swan must have flown through the open doors, Mandy thought. There was a fountain at one end, the end where the Parker Smythes were standing. Mr Parker Smythe had his arm around his wife's shoulder, Mrs Parker Smythe's bright pink lips stretched wide in an ugly shape as she screeched and wailed, and Imogen's hands were clenched into fists and she was holding them to her mouth as she stared with huge eyes at the swan.

'Get it out, Mandy!' cried Mrs Parker Smythe. 'Don't just stand there! Get it out! Ronald, Ronald, tell her to get it out!'

'Mummy, she's going to,' piped Imogen. 'Oh, poor swan. Poor, poor swan! Is it hurt, Mandy?'

Mandy didn't answer. She was planning the best way to approach the swan. She didn't want to panic the bird. One wing seemed to be drooping slightly. But the swan was alive and it was calm. *Too calm*? wondered Mandy. Was it already in shock?

'Get it *out*!' Mrs Parker Smythe screeched again.

Mandy had decided what to do. She'd go down the steps into the pool and get into the water as smoothly as possible. Then she'd glide along and get close to the swan. Then . . . Well, what happened next would depend on how the swan reacted. Mandy put the carrier bag down kicked off her trainers and took off her socks.

'At last!' She's doing something *at last*!' said Mrs Parker Smythe.

'I want to help!' said Imogen as Mandy went down the steps into the pool.

As Imogen stepped towards the pool, Mandy heard Mrs Parker Smythe scream, 'Immie! Immie, my precious, you mustn't!'

The shrill command echoed round Mandy as she glided closer and closer to the swan. And at last she was there.

'It's all right, Swan,' Mandy murmured. 'You'll be all right. Come on, let me see you . . . there, there . . .'

The water wasn't too deep here, but it came up to Mandy's chin as her feet touched the bottom of the pool. She put a hand out and stroked the swan. It turned its head, bent its neck and touched Mandy's face with its bill. And then Mandy noticed the nylon line dangling from the swan's bill. *Fishing-line!* thought Mandy, gazing at it. She wondered if she ought to try and pull it out.

But maybe the swan had swallowed a long length of line. There was a lot of line on a fishing-rod, wasn't there? Even worse, *what if the swan had swallowed a hook?*

The swan moved its bill over Mandy's cheek and Mrs Parker Smythe screamed. 'It's going to attack her! Oh my goodness! What will our guests think when they arrive?'

But the swan stayed calm and placid. It was in the centre of the pool, though; Mandy wondered how she could get it to the steps at the side. Simon had said she'd have to get the swan out. He hadn't said *how*!

'How can I move you, Swan?' she whispered. 'Shall I try walking backwards and pulling? No! That's be no good, would it! I might hurt you!'

Mandy frowned. If pulling wasn't the answer . . . maybe *pushing* was. 'All right, Swan,' she murmured. 'Let's give it a try. I'm going to swim up behind you, put one arm either side of your body and guide you to the steps. OK?'

Mandy took a deep breath to calm herself; the swan might not like what she was about to do. She knew it might turn round and swipe her with its one strong wing.

But the swan seemed to understand that Mandy was helping it. It allowed itself to be gently pushed and guided towards the steps. The Parker Smythes were silent now; the only sound in the pool room was that of a gentle splashing, as Mandy slowly kicked her feet behind her.

Then Imogen called softly, 'Keep going, Mandy. You've nearly made it!'

And they were there; they'd made it to the steps. Mandy manoeuvred the swan to the side of them. She stood on the bottom step and looked at the bird. One wing was still drooping, but she'd have to take a chance and hope she didn't damage the wing any more when she lifted the swan. Now she'd got this far, she didn't dare waste time asking one of the Parker Smythes to fetch a towel to wrap round the swan! Not yet!

Simon's instructions played themselves over in Mandy's mind. 'Take its head in one hand . . . put your other arm round its body . . . be careful not to miss its wings . . .'

The swan was surprisingly heavy. It was

awkward lifting it sideways, trying to support it and herself at the same time. And its long neck was in front of her eyes, blocking her vision.

I'll just have to feel for the steps with my feet! thought Mandy, trying not to admit to herself that she was terrified in case she tripped and dropped the swan, or fell on top of it!

Somehow, Mandy managed – though she stumbled slightly when she reached the top step and bent to place the swan on the white marble pool surround. It was now, for the first time, that Mandy noticed the bald patches on top of the swan's head.

It must be one of the new swans from the river, Mandy thought as she called urgently to Imogen. 'Will you bring that carrier bag I put down over there, Imogen? Be careful, there's medicine in it for the swan.'

'Immie! Immie!' Mrs Parker Smythe came back to life. 'Don't go near that bird! It might be dangerous . . . it might have creepy-crawlies on it. Oh, look!' her voice rose to a wail. 'It's making a *mess* on my marble tiles. We'll have to disinfect!'

Mr Parker Smythe didn't say anything.

'Ronald. Did you hear me? We'll have to disinfect. Where's Mrs Bates? She's never

around when she's needed! Go and fetch her
to clean the tiles, Ronald. Immie! Immie!'
she commanded again. 'Don't go near that
swan!'

Imogen completely ignored her mother. She
walked slowly but determinedly towards Mandy
and the swan. Then she stood next to Mandy
and said quietly, 'Shall I get the medicine out?'

Mandy nodded. She kept her eyes on what
she was doing. The swan had sunk down onto
the marble tiles, long neck and one wing
drooping and the nylon line dangling from its
bill. Mandy was tugging very gently at the line,
but it was no good; it wouldn't move. She'd have
to leave it. She could see the swan's body moving
as it breathed. And it seemed to be breathing
very fast.

Mandy heard the rustling of the carrier bag,
then the rustling of a paper bag as Imogen
undid it. 'Here, Mandy,' she said softly.

Her eyes still on the swan, Mandy held out a
hand and Imogen put the small phial of glucose
solution and the syringe on to it.

Over by the fountain, Mrs Parker Smythe was
moaning to herself. Mandy didn't spare her a
glance. Carefully, she filled the syringe. 'I'm
going to make the swan open her beak and try

and dribble some of this into her mouth,' she said. 'Move back now, Imogen.'

'No, I'll hold the squirter thing while you open its beak,' said Imogen. 'I'll be careful, Mandy. 'I won't let any of the medicine come out.'

Mandy bit her lip. It *would* be easier if Imogen held the syringe. She decided to chance it.

Mandy passed her the syringe. Speaking softly and soothingly to the swan, she opened its beak the way Simon had told her to. Imogen moved closer and put the syringe into Mandy's spare hand. Mandy pressed gently on the plunger and carefully dribbled a couple of drops into the swan's mouth.

'Swallow it. Please swallow it,' whispered Mandy. 'It will do you good.'

The swan did swallow it. Mandy smiled and asked Imogen to dribble a few more drops into its mouth. Again, the swan swallowed, but after that she didn't seem to want any more.

'Well, you've had quite a bit,' said Mandy. 'It should help.'

But when Mandy took her fingers from round its bill, the swan's head and neck drooped once more.

Mr Parker Smythe returned, but without the housekeeper. 'Your mother has just phoned,' he said to Mandy. 'She'll be here in ten minutes.'

Mandy nodded. The swan's breathing was slower. Was it too slow? It looked very weak and feeble. Maybe if she could get the bird down to the gates, be there when her mum arrived, it would save a bit of precious time. But this time she'd better make sure the swan wouldn't be able to move its wings; it wouldn't do for it to struggle and cause more damage to the injured wing.

'Will you get me a towel to wrap round the swan, Imogen?' she asked.

Once again, Mrs Parker Smythe came to life. 'Find Mrs Bates and ask her for an *old* towel, Immie darling. Oh, no, the horrible thing has made another mess!'

'Old towel!' muttered Mr Parker Smythe. 'Really! What will one towel matter? You stay here, Imogen. I'll see to this!' He turned and moved away.

Mandy stroked the swan, silently begging it to keep breathing, to stay alive.

Mr Parker Smythe wasn't long, but he *seemed* to be gone for ages. When he reappeared he was carrying two towels. 'One for you and one for the swan,' he told Mandy.

'Thank you,' Mandy murmured, taking the

neatly folded, soft towels from him. She put one towel on the floor, and, as she wrapped the other one around the swan she noticed the navy-blue initials, "PS", embroidered on each corner.

Mrs Parker Smythe shrieked loudly. 'Ronald! They are our *new* towels! I ordered them especially for our guests. They're embroidered with real silk!'

'Mandy, my dear,' said Mr Parker Smythe, 'I must apologise for my wife. I'm afraid she always gets a bit edgy when we're expecting guests!' Mandy was almost sure Mr Parker Smythe winked as he picked up the second towel and wrapped it round her shoulders. 'Hang on a minute, I'll get your trainers,' he added.

'Thank you,' muttered Mandy. She pushed her feet into them, then stooped to lift the swan. It felt heavier than ever. Her effort must have tired her more than she'd realised.

Then she heard running footsteps and voices. 'It's James, James and . . . Mum!' she whispered thankfully, smiling weakly as Emily Hope rushed towards her.

'I'd better go over and try to calm my wife down,' said Mr Parker Smythe, moving away.

'All right, Mandy!' said Mrs Hope. 'Let me take the swan, love.'

'Imogen helped me give it some glucose, Mum but I don't know if it's still alive!' Mandy gave a choke of emotion as Mrs Hope carefully lifted the swan from her.

'It *is* alive, Mandy,' James said reassuringly. 'Its eyes are moving.'

'I think it's one of the new swans from the river, James,' said Mandy as they hurried out of the pool room and along the path. 'The one who hissed at us.'

'Well, if it is that one, it won't give up easily!' said James with a smile.

When they reached the front drive, Imogen darted ahead and opened the back door of the Land-rover. Mandy and James climbed in and Mrs Hope carefully put the swan in between them.

'Don't worry, Swan!' said Imogen. 'You'll soon get better at Animal Ark.' She looked anxiously at Mrs Hope. 'She will, won't she?'

'I hope so!' Emily Hope smiled at the little girl as she shut the door and moved swiftly round the vehicle. 'We'll let you know when there's any news, Imogen.'

Seven

'OK, Mandy?' asked Mrs Hope, glancing over the seat as she got into the Land-rover.

'Yes, she's nice and secure,' replied Mandy. The swan had stretched her neck out and was resting it over Mandy's knees. 'What about this nylon fishing-line, Mum? How will you get it out? There might be hooks on the other end of it.'

'Don't worry. We'll find a way,' said Mrs Hope as she started the vehicle. 'The main thing is you managed to get the swan out of the swimming-pool and to give her some glucose. It's really all you could have done given the circumstances.'

'I wish I'd been there to help you, Mandy,' said James. 'I would have been if Mum and Dad hadn't dropped me off in Walton on the way back from Sheffield. I had to call in at the bike shop.'

'Oh, heck! I've left my bike at the Parker Smythes'!' said Mandy. 'And where's yours, James?'

'At home. I haven't been back yet. Your mum spotted me getting off the bus outside the Fox and Goose,' explained James. 'She knew I'd want to see the swan.'

'Dad or I will pick your bike up later, Mandy,' said Mrs Hope.

'One of the Parker Smythes might bring it,' said James. 'It's the least they could do. They didn't seem to be helping you at all, Mandy.'

'*Mr* Parker Smythe was OK. He had his hands full with his wife. If I hadn't got the swan out of the pool, I think Mrs Parker Smythe would have gone into shock herself! And Imogen was a big help,' Mandy said.

'It's a good job she was there,' said James. Mandy nodded. She was feeling a little bit better, now that they were on their way to Animal Ark.

'Nearly there,' said Mrs Hope, glancing in her mirror again and noting with relief that some of the colour had returned to Mandy's cheeks.

As they drew up to Animal Ark, Adam Hope came round the corner of the cottage, pulling on a white surgery coat as he hurried towards them. 'I've only just got back from my meeting,' he said. 'Luckily, the surgery is quiet for once. Now, let's have a look.'

'I think she's hurt one of her wings, Dad,' Mandy told him as he lifted the swan. Then she pointed to the fishing-line. 'I didn't really try to move that in case there were any hooks on the other end of it.'

Adam Hope nodded and strode away.

'Front way in for you, Mandy,' said Mrs Hope. 'You're to go straight upstairs for a warm bath. No arguing,' she added firmly. 'You need to get out of those wet clothes.'

Mandy didn't linger in the bath; she was too anxious to hear what her parents had to say about the swan. She got dressed quickly and hurried downstairs.

'Your mum said we can go through to the surgery after you've drunk this,' said James, handing Mandy a mug of tea.

'That's good,' said Mandy. 'Mum must think the swan's going to be OK if she said that. But

I can't *begin* to think how they'll get that fishing-line out. And what will they do if her wing's broken?'

'We'll find out when we go through to them,' said James. 'I've put plenty of milk in your tea so you can drink it quickly,' she added. Mandy smiled. James was a really good friend.

There was nobody in the waiting area when Mandy and James went through to the surgery. 'Wow! It is quiet for a Saturday!' said Mandy. 'Are Mum, Dad and Simon with the swan, Jean?'

The receptionist shook her head. 'Your mother's with Elise Knight. She brought Maisy in to have her stitches checked. And any time now Mrs Ponsonby will be here with Pandora and Toby. They're due for their injections. But your father and Simon are in the annexe with the swan.'

'Thanks, Jean,' said Mandy. 'We'll go in to them.'

The annexe had been set up especially for the wild animals that were treated at Animal Ark. They had to be kept separate from domestic animals to avoid any cross-infection. Mandy found white coats for herself and James and they hurried in. Simon was holding the swan steady on a small treatment table.

'How is she?' Mandy asked, walking quietly over to them.

'Fair,' replied Simon. 'Fair.'

'*Is* it a she, Simon?' asked James.

'Yes, she's a pen,' Simon nodded. 'A year, maybe two years old, I should think.'

'Hello, girl,' Mandy whispered. 'Are you OK, then?'

'She's damaged the muscles and tendons of the top bone in her right wing,' said Simon. 'My guess is that she flew into something. Maybe during this morning's storm.'

'Or maybe she was panicking because she'd swallowed the fishing-line,' said Mandy.

'Mmm, that's possible,' Simon agreed. 'We've given her a couple of injections,' he continued. 'One for shock, and an antibiotic to prevent infection. Her wing isn't cut but it's grazed and bruised.'

'What about the fishing-line?' asked Mandy.

'We're about to remove it,' said Adam Hope as he came towards them. 'We X-rayed her to see if she'd swallowed any lead weights or hooks, but I couldn't see any,' he added. 'So it should be fairly straightforward. We'll have to sedate her, though.'

Mandy let out a small sigh. That probably

meant she and James would have to wait outside.

But Mr Hope glanced thoughtfully at them. 'James, do you think you could come here and keep her body steady? And, Mandy, you support her neck. Keep it as straight and upright as possible, OK?'

Mandy and James nodded eagerly, thrilled that Mr Hope was letting them help. But as soon as he'd checked the instrument trolley with Simon, he told them to move away.

'You can stand over there and watch,' he said. 'But keep still and don't speak. We'll explain what we're doing as we go along.'

Mandy and James nodded and Mr Hope continued quietly, 'First, I'm going to put a little rubber mask over the swan's nostrils and bill. Then . . .' he pointed to a tube that was attached to the mask, 'I'll send a small amount of sleeping gas through here. It'll only take a couple of minutes or so to send her to sleep.'

Then Simon explained what would happen when the swan was asleep. 'Mr Hope will put an endoscope down the swan's throat,' he said. 'It's a sort of long flexible tube with a lens on one end. It will let him see how much line the swan has swallowed. He'll also be able to see where the line is and if it's twisted round or knotted.'

'OK, Simon!' Mr Hope said. 'She's asleep. Here we go.'

Simon moved close to the instrument trolley.

Mr Hope put out a hand and Simon put the endoscope and another instrument into it. 'Endoscope and forceps,' he told James and Mandy.

'Forceps act like tweezers,' said Mr Hope. 'I'll feed them down alongside the endoscope . . . There's a little hook-like thing on the endoscope tube to hold it in place.'

James and Mandy's eyes were glued to the vet's hands as, with deft, sure movements, playing the tube out bit by bit, he eased the endoscope and the forceps down the swan's throat. *I just hope I'll be as good a vet as Dad one day*, thought Mandy as she watched him put his eye to the lens in order to see all the way down the swan's throat.

'As soon as your dad has seen exactly where the line is, he'll use the tweezers to get hold of it,' Simon explained to Mandy. 'Then, while I guide the line from this end, he can gently pull the line from where it is inside the swan, watching through the lens to make sure it doesn't tangle itself round anything, or snap, or cut into the bird's throat on its way up. It should only take a couple of minutes.'

Hardly breathing, James and Mandy watched the practice nurse and vet intently. Very soon Mr Hope was holding up a long length of nylon line for them to see.

Three or four minutes after that, the swan started to come round. James's glasses had slid right to the end of his nose. Until now, he hadn't dared to push them back into place.

Then, to Mandy's delight, the swan gave a small but unmistakable *hiss-sss*.

'I should think she'll have a bit of a sore throat,' said Simon, and the swan hissed gently again.

'That settles it,' said Mandy, walking over and stroking the swan's chest. 'We'll call her Sally!'

Adam Hope stroked his beard thoughtfully. 'There'll have been chlorine in the swimming pool water. I don't think it will do any harm but, while she's still a bit dopey, we may as well give her a light sponge down.'

Mandy looked at her father pleadingly and he smiled. 'All right, you and James can do that,' he said. 'Afterwards, though, she'll need complete rest and peace and quiet for twelve hours.'

So Mandy and James gently sponged Sally's

chest and body and after that Mr Hope carried her over to a large cage. As he closed the door, she looked up and hissed again. 'There, she's thanking you, Dad,' said Mandy.

'If you'd seen the look in her beady eyes you wouldn't be thinking that!' chuckled Adam Hope. 'Come on, we'll leave her to rest now.'

When Mandy and James went back to the reception area, Mrs Ponsonby was by the desk talking to Mrs Hope and Jean. Pandora, her chubby Pekinese, and Toby the lovable mongrel, pulled eagerly at their leads. They knew Mandy and James would come and make a fuss of them.

As they bent to stroke the dogs, Mrs Ponsonby turned and said, 'I suppose you two don't know anything about the plants that have suddenly appeared in the village pond?'

'Plants, Mrs Ponsonby?' Do you mean pond plants?' asked James, innocently.

'Is that what everybody was looking at earlier on?' said Mandy. 'I saw a little crowd of people standing round the pond when I was on my way to Beacon House.'

'Somebody put them there,' said Mrs Ponsonby. 'And I'll find out who it was. You can be sure of that!' The daisies on her big straw hat bobbed up and down as she nodded her head. Mandy caught her mother's eye and had to hide a smile. Emily Hope knew that James and Mandy had neatly avoided answering Mrs Ponsonby's question.

'Well, we haven't actually seen the plants in the pond, so we don't know if they're the ones Philip Meakin brought,' Mandy said after Mrs Ponsonby had marched regally out of the door. 'I mean, I gave those plants to Walter, didn't I?' she added mischievously.

'Mandy Hope! You're impossible!' said Mrs Hope, her eyes sparkling as she shook her head. 'Anyway, how did things go with the swan?'

'We've called her Sally,' said Mandy. 'Pronounced Ssssally, 'cos she hisses.'

'It was terrific, Mrs Hope,' said James. 'Mr Hope let us watch while he pulled the fishing-line out.'

'Then James and I sponged her down,' added Mandy. 'We've got to leave her to rest now until tomorrow. Oh, and she's damaged muscles and tendons in her wing, Mum.'

Mrs Hope nodded. 'I'll go and have a word with your dad in a minute,' she said. 'Don't make any plans to go anywhere this evening, Mandy. Gran and Grandad have invited us to a barbecue. I said we'd take some salad and dips. Perhaps you could make a start on them? You and Blackie are invited to the barbecue as well, James,' she added with a smile.

'Blackie too? Are you sure, Mrs Hope?'

'Gran says he'll save her from having to pick up crumbs and leftovers afterwards,' Emily Hope chuckled.

'Wow! Thanks. We'll be there!' said James, his eyes bright.

Mrs Hope chuckled again and went off to see her husband.

'I love barbecues,' said Mandy, 'but I wanted to see if the other new swan is still on the river. I won't have time to go if I'm making the salad and dips.'

'I could go though,' said James. 'I'll go home first and fetch Blackie. He'll enjoy a walk by the river. I'll make it a long one, then he'll be too tired to misbehave himself at your gran's!'

'Good idea,' Mandy agreed with a laugh. 'I'll see you later at Lilac Cottage, then.'

Mandy stayed to chat with Jean for a while, then her parents appeared with Simon. Mandy noticed they all looked serious. 'What's the matter?' she asked in alarm. 'Sally's all right, isn't she?'

'As far as we can tell, she is, Mandy,' replied Adam Hope. 'But . . .'

'We're not too happy about her wing,' said Mrs Hope. 'There's a chance we might have to amputate it.'

Mandy thought of the journey Sally had made; flying and swooping her way to Welford to make a new home. She remembered the way Sally had risen up in the river, spreading her magnificent wings wide. Her face clouded. 'Oh, no,' she said sadly. 'That would be terrible! Poor Sally!' Mandy sighed and shook her head. 'But why? Why might Sally have to lose her wing? Is it broken, after all?'

'Remember I told you that she'd damaged the muscles and tendons of the top wing bone, Mandy?' said Simon. 'Well, if there's too much damage to the muscles she'll never be able to hold her wing in place.'

'That means the wing would start to droop even more,' said Mrs Hope. 'It would drag along the ground and the tip of the wing would get damaged and infected.'

'But you'd only have to amputate if the muscles *are* too badly damaged?' Mandy asked hopefully.

'Yes. And we think the odds are slightly in

Sally's favour, Mandy.' Mr Hope gave a small smile. 'She seems quite a strong and healthy bird. That *should* help the healing process. It will be a while before we know one way or the other,' Mr Hope ruffled her hair. 'But we wanted you to be prepared, just in case.'

Mandy nodded. Her parents were always up front with her. Sometimes, though, the truth hurt. 'I'll go and start the salad,' she said. 'It might take my mind off it for a while.'

Eight

When James arrived at Lilac Cottage, Mandy's grandad and Reverend Hadcroft were cooking the food, Emily Hope was carrying a tray of iced drinks towards Mandy's gran who was chatting to Flo Maynard and, nearby, Adam Hope was deep in conversation with Philip Meakin from the garden centre.

Then James saw Mandy at the bottom of the garden and started to make his way towards her. She was watching Smoky, her grandparents' young cat, climbing up a tree.

'Don't you dare bark at Smoky!' James said sternly to Blackie, as they got closer.

Mandy turned round to greet Blackie,

laughing when he jumped up excitedly and tried to lick her face. 'I've already had a wash, you licky dog,' she told him. Then she looked across at James. 'Look what Flo Maynard's brought, James. A reed collar for Smoky to wear at the procession. I wanted to try it on him but he ran off and started to climb that tree!'

'I wonder if Flo would make a few more,' James said, as he examined the collar. 'It'd look good if some of the other animals wore collars, too.'

'She's already offered,' said Mandy. 'She says they don't take her very long to make. I think you're next on her list for one, Blackie!' she added, patting his big head.

Blackie barked loudly, then ran back up the garden to where the food was being cooked. James laughed. 'He's far more interested in seeing what might fall off the grill than hearing about what he's going to wear to the procession.'

'Mmm,' Mandy agreed. She was watching Blackie but she wasn't laughing or even smiling. Then she turned to look at James. 'Sally might have to have her wing amputated, James,' she said miserably.

'Why? Is it broken after all?' he asked, aghast.

'No, it isn't broken. But . . .' Mandy went on

to tell him what her parents and Simon had said earlier.

'So what would happen to her in the end?' asked James. 'She won't be able to go back in the wild if she can't fly, will she?'

'We'd have to find a bird sanctuary for her,' Mandy said gloomily. 'I phoned Betty Hilder, and she said the nearest one is miles away.' Betty ran the Welford Animal Sanctuary but she only took in small birds.

'Well, at least Sally is going to live, Mandy,' said James. 'That's something. She'd probably settle down happily enough at a sanctuary specially for birds. And even if we couldn't see her, maybe we could adopt her,' he smiled triumphantly. 'You know, Mandy, pay a little bit each month between us towards her keep and—'

'James, that's a brilliant idea!' Mandy interrupted. 'Then of course, Sally might *not* have to lose her wing. It might heal and then she can go back to the river. We'll have to wait and see. And,' she added more cheerfully, 'at least waiting and seeing means she'll have to stay at Animal Ark for a while.'

James nodded then sniffed the air loudly. 'Now that *that*'s sorted out . . . he said meaningfully.

'OK, I get the message,' laughed Mandy. 'Let's go and get some food. But James, there's something else staying at Animal Ark for a while, too. Philip Meakin phoned to ask if he could bring another one of his lizards in on his way here. He was cleaning the vivarium out when he noticed a nasty abscess on its tummy. Anyway, Mum's decided to keep her under observation for a couple of days. Her name's Lizzie, she's a leopard gecko. Her markings are fantastic, just like a leopard's.'

Mandy paused for breath then said, 'And guess what, James? Tomorrow, Reverend Hadcroft's going to make a special announcement about the procession and animal service.'

'Wow, that's good!' said James. 'Is there any more startling news or . . .' he rubbed his tummy and grinned, 'or can I eat now?'

'Well,' said Mandy, 'Flo Maynard's coming towards us. I think she wants a word with you about Blackie's reed collar, James. You talk to her and I'll get the food.'

'Here you are, Mandy, love!' Grandad smiled as she hurried up to the grill. 'The veggie-burgers are ready and waiting for you.'

Mandy smiled back; she didn't eat meat if she could help it. 'Thanks, Grandad,' she said, moving the salad to one side to make room for the burgers.

'I'll put an extra sausage on James's plate for Blackie,' he said. 'He's being very-well behaved this evening. He's hardly left my side.'

'The thought of a sausage or a bit of chicken falling to the ground works wonders,' chuckled Mandy. 'Though Blackie could be tired. I think James took him for a long walk before they got here. Which reminds me, there's something I must ask James.'

As Mandy handed James his plate she said, 'You haven't told me yet if you saw Sally's friend on the river.'

'I didn't see any of the swans,' said James. 'There were about two dozen ducks there, though. Blackie was going bananas because I wouldn't let him chase them.' He paused to eat some food, then went on, 'There were two strangers walking along the riverbank, too. I think they might have been judges doing a spot check. I heard one of them say something about going to the Fox and Goose to see how friendly the locals were.'

'I'm sure they'll have found a grand welcome,' said Gran. 'And the outside of the Fox and Goose looks a picture! Walter Pickard and

Grandad spent half the afternoon putting up hanging flower baskets. That should add a good few points to our score.'

'And then there are those mysterious plants that have suddenly grown in the village pond, too,' Mandy added with a chuckle.

'I heard about them,' said Gran, her eyes twinkling. 'I think by the time of the next meeting, there might be a few more people agreeing that plants are the best idea for the pond. In fact, it might be an idea to ask Philip if he'll write out a list of suitable plants and give us an idea of what they'd cost.'

'He could bring it with him when he comes to fetch Lizzie,' said Mandy. 'You'll have to come and see her tomorrow, James. She really is lovely.'

'I will,' said James. 'And we'll be able to visit Sally tomorrow, won't we?'

'Yes, if Mum and Dad say it's OK,' said Mandy. 'They might think she needs to be left alone a while longer. But we'll go down to the river again to see if we can find her friend. I hope she's not hurt, too.'

Emily Hope walked up to them with a tray of glasses. 'I think you're looking for an excuse to bring another swan to Animal Ark, Mandy,' she said teasingly. 'Oh, and I didn't get round to telling you earlier; Elise wondered if you and James would call in tomorrow. Maisy was fine when I checked her over. It'll do her no harm to start a gentle training programme. I think Elise might appreciate some help, though.'

Mandy nodded. 'I told her we'd help. I'm glad she's taken me up on my offer.'

Soon after that, the party broke up.

'Almost the end of a very busy day,' said Adam Hope, smiling contentedly at his wife and daughter as he locked the garage door on Animal Ark's Land-rover.

'And tomorrow will be another busy day,' said Mandy. 'James and I have got loads to do. Dad, *how* long will it be before you know about Sally's wing?' she added anxiously once they were inside.

'I'm not sure, Mandy,' admitted Mr Hope, stroking his beard thoughtfully. 'Once we start letting her move around a bit, we might have a better idea. We'll be able to see how well she holds her wing while she's walking. It's hard to judge properly when she's in a confined space.'

'It'll be a few days anyway, Mandy,' said Emily Hope. 'Muscles take time to heal. At this stage we really can't tell how severe the damage is.'

'What about feeding her?' asked Mandy. 'She'll need more than bread. What do swans eat?'

'Mainly water weeds and other vegetation,' replied Mrs Hope. 'And maybe the odd small frog. But we'll give her a diet of corn, flaked maize and lettuce, and put her on a course of multi-vitamin capsules to make up for anything lacking.'

'You can help me work out a feeding sheet tomorrow, Mandy,' said Adam Hope, ruffling her hair. 'But now . . . you're looking very tired, and I wouldn't mind an earlyish night myself.'

'I *am* tired now I come to think about it,' said Mandy. And, yawning hugely, she said good-night and went up to bed.

For once, Mandy woke up late. She lay for a while and watched the sunbeams dancing over the posters on her bedroom walls, then she recognised her mum's footsteps on the stairs.

'Morning, Mum!' she called, sitting up. 'Have you seen Sally this morning. How is she?'

'Morning, Mandy.' Mrs Hope came in, looking serious. 'It isn't very good news, I'm afraid.' She sat on the edge of the bed and looked at her daughter.

'You mean her wing, Mum? Is it worse?'

'It's difficult to say. The trouble is . . .' Emily Hope shook her head, her green eyes were worried, '. . . Sally doesn't seem able to get onto her feet,' she said quietly.

'Maybe Sally's wing is really painful and she knows it would hurt even more if she stood up,' suggested Mandy. 'Or maybe she feels stiff because she hasn't been able to move around very much. Could that be it, Mum?'

'Yes,' replied Emily Hope. 'It could be something like that. Or . . .' her brow creased as she thought, '. . . it could be post-trauma debility; that's a sort of delayed shock.'

'Has she eaten anything?' Mandy asked as she got out of bed.

'We haven't tried to feed her yet.' Mrs Hope smiled. 'We're saving that job for you.'

'Great!' said Mandy. 'I'll have a shower and be down in a few minutes.'

Mrs Hope insisted on Mandy eating breakfast before she went through to the annexe. Mandy sighed; she was longing to go to Sally, but she knew it was no use arguing. Orange juice, a bowl of cereal and two slices of toast disappeared rapidly.

As she made her way through the surgery, Mandy heard her dad's voice. He was saying something in a gentle, encouraging tone. And when she entered the annexe, Mandy saw that he'd got Sally out of the large cage.

The swan's body had sunk to the floor, her back towards Mandy. She was holding her injured wing at an awkward angle and her long neck was drooping. Sally looked like a large, white, huddled shape of misery. Mandy felt a lump form in her throat.

'Good morning, Mandy,' Adam Hope said quietly, without looking up. 'I thought if I got her out it might encourage her to stand. But either she can't or she doesn't want to. I'm not sure which.'

Mandy moved slowly round to the front of the swan. 'Hello, Sally,' she murmured as she knelt down. 'What's the matter then, is your wing hurting?'

Sally lifted her neck slightly then stretched it out towards Mandy. She blinked her beady eyes. Then she made a soft little trumpeting note, stretched her neck further and rested her head on Mandy's shoulder.

'Who's a sad swan, then?' whispered Mandy, running gentle fingers down Sally's neck and

stroking her chest feathers. The swan honked twice and banged her orange bill against Mandy's ear. Then she made a small whistling noise. 'I think she's asking for something to eat,' said Mandy. Sally whistled again.

'I can't think why this breed is known as the *mute* swan,' said Adam Hope, smiling down at them. 'I wonder if they're all as talkative as this young lady! I think we'll try her on a small bowl of bran mash with some lettuce chopped up in it, Mandy.'

'OK,' said Mandy, starting to get up.

Sally didn't seem to like Mandy moving away.

She gave a distressed little cry and pushed her neck out to its full length, trying to reach Mandy.

'She seems to want you to stay around,' said Mr Hope. 'I'll make her breakfast on my own.'

'How about carrying her outside into the garden, Dad?' Mandy asked thoughtfully. 'Maybe she doesn't like the idea of walking on tiles.'

'You might have a point there, Mandy,' Emily Hope had come quietly into the annexe just in time to hear Mandy's suggestion. 'I'll carry her out, though. I don't want you lifting her and straining yourself.'

Mrs Hope placed Sally carefully in the centre of the lawn, then moved away from her. And, although the swan circled her long neck to look round, she remained where Mrs Hope had put her, with her lower chest and tummy sunk close to the ground.

Mandy called her, then walked in front of her and all round her in a large circle. But the swan didn't even try to get up. 'Maybe she'll try later,' said Mandy. 'After she's had something to eat.'

'Maybe,' Emily Hope nodded but she didn't look too hopeful. 'You stay and talk to her while Dad's making her breakfast, Mandy. Give her some of your famous TLC.'

James came by a few minutes later to find

Mandy and Sally sitting together on the lawn.

'You're just in time to help me feed her, James,' said Mandy.

'Is she OK? What about her wing?' James crouched down in front of Sally and looked sideways at her wing. 'It's still drooping a bit, isn't it?'

Mandy sighed, 'And Sally can't seem to get on to her feet, James. Mum and Dad don't know why. I was hoping it might have been because she didn't want to walk on the tiled floor, but . . .' Mandy sighed again, '. . . she hasn't even attempted to get up now we're here.'

'Her bad wing doesn't stop her moving her neck,' said James, leaning back slightly as Sally stretched it towards him. 'Oh, cripes,' he whispered, as the swan reached for his face to tap his glasses with her bill.

'It's OK, she's ever so gentle when she does that,' Mandy assured him. 'Aren't you, Sally-girl?'

Sally removed her bill from James's face, looked at Mandy and made her honking noise. Mandy honked back and Sally lifted her neck to its full height and looked down at her.

'She's trying to work out if you're a swan, too,' chuckled James.

Mr Hope arrived in a hurry, carrying a large dish with Sally's food in and a bucket of water. 'We'll have to leave you to it, Mandy,' he said. 'There's an emergency up at Burnside Farm; one of Mr Matthews' cows has fallen into a disused water lodge. We're both going. Here's the cordless phone, I've got my mobile, ring me if anyone else needs us.'

'OK, Dad.' Mandy didn't waste time asking any questions; she knew it must be really serious if both her parents were going.

'Look, Mandy!' said James. 'Sally's trying to reach her food. That must be a good sign.'

Mandy nodded then moved closer and held the dish towards the swan. Without hesitation, Sally dipped her bill into the food and began to suck and slurp happily.

'She wouldn't act like this if she were in shock, would she?' asked James.

'I wouldn't have thought so,' said Mandy. 'But Mum said it might be a sort of delayed shock – post-trauma debility she called it. I don't know what that means exactly, I think it's a sort of weakness that comes on after a fright.'

'That's probably it.' James nodded. 'And poor Sally had more than one fright. I wonder how long the weakness lasts.'

'If food makes it better she'll soon be OK,' said Mandy, tilting the dish so Sally could reach the last of the bran mash.

But, suddenly, Sally lifted her head from the dish and shook her head from side to side. Then she started to make funny bubbling noises as though she were fighting for breath.

'Mandy! What's wrong with her?' asked James in alarm.

'I don't know!' gasped Mandy. 'I'll try and hold her head still, James, and you rub her neck and throat.'

After a bit of a struggle, Mandy managed to grasp Sally's head firmly. Gingerly, James ran his fingers down the length of the swan's neck, then moved them up again to where he guessed her throat was. He made gentle little circling movements; Sally snuffled and bubbled even more.

'What shall we do?' said Mandy. 'I don't really want to phone Dad. But . . .' She looked worriedly at poor Sally. 'James, I think she's choking!'

Nine

'Let's try Simon!' said James, picking up the cordless phone. 'You know the number at his flat, don't you?'

'Yes, Walton 887770,' said Mandy. 'You do it, James. I want to keep Sally's head up and her neck straight if I can.'

Mandy waited tensely to see if Simon answered and let her breath out with a relieved sigh when James started speaking.

James quickly explained the situation, murmuring, 'Yes . . . OK . . . Right,' at intervals. Finally he said, 'We'll see you soon, then, Simon. Thanks.' He pressed the off button and said quickly, 'He'll get here as soon as he can.

Meanwhile, we need cotton-wool buds, Mandy.'

'Dressing trolley in the treatment room,' she told him. James was on the move before she'd finished speaking.

'We need to try and clean the swan's nostrils,' James said when he returned. 'Simon says they'll be blocked with food.'

'OK,' said Mandy, still holding Sally's head. 'Do you want to try it, James?'

James nodded, pushing his glasses further back on his nose. 'Keep still, Sally,' he implored the swan. 'I'm going to put this in your nostril and clear your nose passage.'

Sally struggled at first, then she seemed to understand James was trying to help her. Mandy made soothing noises and handed James fresh cotton buds when he needed them.

'The bubbling noise isn't as bad now, James,' she said quietly. 'I think it's working.'

James nodded. 'I'll do the other nostril now,' he said, moving carefully round to the other side of Mandy. Sally gave a small hiccup and then made a noise like a dog sneezing. 'That's right,' said James, 'good swan. That's helping to get rid of the gunge. Now let me clear a bit more out.'

Mandy's arms were aching terribly by this

time; she wriggled herself a bit closer to Sally and tried to reposition herself. James carried on, carefully removing the caked food. 'Trickiest bit now,' he said, standing back and wiping his brow. 'Simon said once it was done, it would be a good idea to blow down each nostril hole to remove the last bits. But he said to be very careful and to watch she doesn't turn nasty.'

'I'll do it,' said Mandy. 'I'll blow gently into her face for a bit first, to get her used to it.'

'Good idea,' James agreed. 'I'll keep her steady from the back.' He placed one hand either side of the swan's body, on top of her wings. Then he stretched his head and neck to one side so he'd be able to watch Mandy.

'You look like you're trying to imitate Sally,' Mandy giggled.

Sally gave a small honk. 'Clever girl, you've learned how to laugh,' said Mandy, moving her face closer to the swan's.

James watched anxiously as Mandy pursed her lips and started to blow softly into Sally's face.

Sally blinked and pushed her bill under Mandy's chin. 'She likes it, don't you Sally?' Mandy cooed.

Mandy blew again; Sally jerked her head back and hissed: *Ssssa! Ssssa!*

'Careful, Mandy,' whispered James.

'It's OK, it was a friendly hiss,' murmured Mandy. 'I'm going to chance it now, James. 'I'm going to blow into her nostril.' Mandy took a deep breath, put her lips to Sally's nostril hole and blew slowly but quite hard. Then she lifted her face and stepped back. Sally wriggled around a bit, jerked her head and looked indignant. But she didn't seem worried or upset, so Mandy moved forward and did the same thing to Sally's other nostril.

'There, Sally,' she said. 'Is that better now?'

Sally replied with a whole series of noises, grunts, honks, trumpets and whistles. James stumbled backwards in surprise and yelled as he just missed ending up sitting in the bucket of water!

Sally swung her neck round and looked beady-eyed at him over her folded wings. That made James laugh so hard, he couldn't get up. 'Look at her, Mandy!' he gasped.

Mandy made her way round to the back of Sally. The swan was still staring at James. 'Oh, I wish I'd got a camera,' said Mandy, kneeling down beside James to watch what Sally would do next.

'Simon said to give her a drink of water when

we'd cleaned her nostrils,' said James after he'd stopped laughing.

'And I think I can hear Simon now, driving up the lane,' said Mandy. 'Yes, it's him all right. I'd recognise the sound of his van anywhere.'

James scrambled to his feet and went off up the garden and down by the side of the cottage to meet the practice nurse.

'From what James says, you seem to have managed well enough without me,' said Simon, as he walked towards Mandy and the swan.

'Yes, I think she's OK now,' Mandy replied. 'Look, she's just tucked her head into the feathers of her good wing,' Mandy pointed.

Simon nodded, 'It's a swan's favourite position for relaxing,' he said. 'But I'd like to check her over, Mandy. See if you can persuade her to move her neck and head to the front.'

'Sally,' said Mandy, 'this way, girl. Come on, Sally!'

Simon shook his head in amazement as Sally untucked her head and elegantly moved her neck round until she was facing Mandy. 'You seem to have tamed her in no time at all,' he said, walking slowly round to stand beside Mandy.

'She just seems to have taken to me,' said Mandy. 'Maybe she feels grateful in some way.'

'Maybe,' Simon said with a smile. 'Now, Sally, let's have a good look at you.'

James and Mandy watched as Simon carefully checked the swan's nostrils, bill and mouth. 'Yes, they all seem fine,' he said. 'Put the bucket of water in front of her now and let's see if she'll drink.'

James brought the bucket and dipped his hand in the water, splashing it around to show Sally what it was. The swan honked loudly then plunged her head into the bucket.

'There!' said Simon, 'See that? She's sending up streams of bubbles. So her nostrils are definitely clear.'

'But how can we stop the same thing happening again?' asked Mandy.

'And *why* did it happen this time?' said James.

Simon smiled. 'Swans take most of their food underwater,' he said. 'When they bite off pieces of weed, more often than not, there's stuff on the weed they don't want to eat.'

'Like mud and bits of gravel?' asked Mandy. Simon nodded.

'So,' he continued, 'they get rid of what they don't want by sieving it in their bill.'

'You mean they sort of pick off the bits they don't want?' asked James.

'Yes, that's it. They pick off the rubbish then they pass it out through their nostrils by releasing air bubbles. And that's what Sally tried to do with the food you gave her.'

'But she couldn't, because she didn't have her head under water,' said James. 'Does that mean we'll have to put a dish of bran into a bucket of water? Wouldn't the bran just end up turning the water to slosh?'

'I think it probably would,' agreed Simon. 'No, all you need to do is give her a dish of bran mash without the greens in; put the greens in a bucket of water next to the dish and Sally will take turns dipping into each. And if she doesn't,' Simon grinned at Mandy, 'I'm sure you'll soon teach her how to.'

'That's great, Simon. Thanks for coming over to help,' said Mandy. Then she went on to tell him about the emergency up at Burnside Farm.

'I was coming to Welford later on anyway,' said Simon. 'I saw Ernie and Walter last night and they asked if I'd give a hand building the wooden frame for the rushcart. I'm meeting them on the green at two o'clock. So, if you like, I'll stay on here until then. It will save your parents from having to come back if anything crops up.'

'I could go and make us some sandwiches,' said Mandy. 'We could have a picnic lunch out here.'

'That sounds like a good idea,' said James, stretching himself out on the grass.

'I second that,' agreed Simon.

Mandy smiled and started to move away. But she'd gone only a few steps before Sally stretched her neck out and hissed loudly. Then the swan half-lifted her good wing.

James rolled over on to his side. 'Keep moving slowly away, Mandy,' he whispered urgently. 'Sally might get to her feet and try to follow you.'

'Good idea,' said Mandy and she held her hand out towards the swan. 'Come on, Sally,' she urged. '*Ssssa-Sssa-Ssssa!*'

But Sally lowered her wing and her neck and, as she'd done earlier in the annexe, went into a sad huddled shape.

'Oh, Sally,' murmured Mandy, going back to the swan. 'What are we going to do with you?'

Sally lifted her neck and wrapped it firmly round Mandy's.

'Perhaps *I'd* better make the sandwiches,' said

James. He stood up and gave a startled yelp as something leaped over the gate at the bottom of the garden and came hurtling towards them. 'Cripes! It's Maisy! Something's scared her. Try and cut her off, Simon!'

Simon was already on his feet and whipping off his jacket. He lunged forward, holding it out just below knee level. His timing was perfect. Maisy ran straight into the jacket; it covered her eyes and she paused in flight for a second.

James reached out and got his hands round her heaving body. 'OK!' he grunted and Simon snatched the jacket away from her face.

He bent low, took her head in his hands and forced her to look at him. 'It's all right, Maisy. It's all right,' he said.

Mandy let out a sigh of relief as Maisy stopped struggling. She'd felt so helpless just watching. But the whole thing had happened so quickly.

Then they heard pounding footsteps in the back lane. James glanced up, saw Elise and shouted. 'It's OK, Elise. Maisy's here!'

'Oh, thank heavens!' Elise cried. She didn't stop to open the gate; she climbed over it and dashed up the garden.

James half-lifted Maisy as he turned her round

so she could see Elise. Maisy gave a joyful bark and ran to her mistress.

Nearly in tears, Elise bent down to stroke and cuddle her dog. Then, still breathing hard, she took hold of Maisy's collar and walked her up to Simon and James.

'It was magpies!' she explained. 'Maisy was outside the back door, having a drink of water, when two magpies swooped down and started dive-bombing her. Maisy took fright, jumped right over the gate and ran like mad up the lane.'

'Well, she came to the right place,' said Mandy, trying to wriggle away from Sally.

She'd only taken a couple of steps forward when Maisy looked up and saw her. She pulled free of Elise's grip and bounded forward.

'Whoa, Maisy!' laughed Mandy, staggering backwards as the Dalmatian jumped up at her.

'Maisy!' called Elise. 'Mandy, push her down then point to the ground. Make sure she can see you pointing, though.'

Feeling puzzled, Mandy did as Elise had asked.

Maisy stood there, looking up at Mandy and wagging her tail.

'Point to the ground again, Mandy!' said Elise. 'Use a sort of jabbing movement . . . that's it . . .

Look! Look! She's done it! Maisy is sitting. Give her love now, Mandy!'

Mandy grinned and patted and praised Maisy.

'I've been working on that hand signal with her all week,' Elise said happily. 'She started responding to it a couple of days ago. But I didn't know if it would work with someone else using it. The only thing is; once she's sitting, I don't know how to get her to stand!'

At that moment, Sally hissed loudly and stretched her neck, banging her bill hard on Maisy's back.

Maisy stood up and turned round. For a split second the dog and swan were nose to bill. Mandy didn't know what would happen next. Then Sally drew her neck in and Elise darted forward and quickly pulled Maisy away.

'Now you know how to make Maisy stand!' joked Mandy. 'Get Sally to bang her back.'

'Clever Sally!' chuckled James, looking at the swan. Then he gasped and grabbed Simon's arm. 'Simon! Sally's just moved her bad wing a bit. It isn't drooping as much, I'm sure it isn't. Maybe it's going to get better. Maybe she won't have to have it amputated.'

'Do you hear that, Sally?' said Mandy, going to the swan. 'You might be able to go back to the river after all.'

Mandy was so busy stroking Sally's chest, she didn't notice Simon shaking his head. And before he could say anything the phone rang. It was Walter Pickard asking if he could bring Tom along to the surgery. Tom, the fiercest cat in the village, had been attacked by a couple of magpies.

'It must be the same ones who frightened Maisy!' said Simon.

It was another emergency at Animal Ark. Simon got up and hurried towards the surgery.

Ten

It was the middle of the afternoon before Mr and Mrs Hope returned from Burnside Farm. By then, James and Elise had gone home and Simon had gone off to help Walter and Ernie.

'One cow safe and sound,' reported Mrs Hope. 'It was a struggle, though, and it's a bit of a mystery as to how the planks covering the water lodge came to be moved.'

'You look like you've had a nice peaceful time,' said Adam Hope, throwing himself down on the lawn beside Mandy and Sally. The swan was dozing, her head tucked under her wing feathers; but she opened one eye at the sound of Mr Hope's voice.

'That's what *you* think!' Mandy grinned and went on to tell them everything that had happened.

'I should have thought to tell you to give Sally the water at the same time as her food!' groaned Mr Hope. 'But I was in such a hurry to get away.'

'Well, you did have other things on your mind,' said Mandy. 'And James and I managed OK once Simon had told us what to do. In a way it's a good job it happened. It meant Simon was here to help catch Maisy and to see to Tom. He thinks Tom's OK,' she added. 'But he told Walter to bring him back tomorrow just to make sure. And Elise is coming back tomorrow as well. She's bringing Maisy for a training session at three o'clock!'

'*Ssssaaa!*' agreed Sally, waking up and tapping Mandy's head with her bill.

'Are you hungry again, Sally? All right, I'll get you something to eat,' said Mandy, scratching the top of the swan's head.

'Has she tried to get on to her feet at all?' Mr Hope asked, kneeling down to try and look under Sally's body.

'Uh-uh,' Mandy shook her head and watched her dad crawl all the way round the swan. 'Watch out, Dad!' she warned as Mr Hope got towards the front of Sally again. But the warning came too late. Sally swung her neck round and grabbed hold of Mr Hope's beard.

'Hey! That hurts!' he protested, tapping Sally's bill with his finger. 'It isn't funny!' he said indignantly as Mandy and her mother burst out laughing.

'Oh, but it is,' gasped Mandy. 'Let go, Sally. You naughty swan!'

Sally blinked beadily, then let go of Mr Hope's beard and honked a couple of times.

'She's apologising,' chuckled Mrs Hope. 'Come on, Mandy, we'll leave these two to have a chat and I'll help you prepare Sally's food. Then I'm going to have a shower.'

When Mandy returned with a dish of flaked maize, some chopped greenery to put in the bucket of water and a multi-vitamin capsule, Sally had her neck round Mr Hope's shoulders.

'She seems to like doing that,' said Mandy. 'I don't know if it's a sign of affection or if she's making sure she won't be left alone. Just move your shoulder a bit, Dad, so I can reach her bill. I want to open it and pop this capsule in.'

Sally swallowed the capsule with no trouble at all then moved her neck and reached eagerly towards the dish of food.

Mandy let her eat a small amount then removed the dish and put the bucket in its place. The swan dipped her head below the surface, slurped and bubbled a few times then lifted her head and looked round for the dish. Mandy put it next to the bucket.

'Well, she's soon learned the correct way of doing it,' said Adam Hope as they watched the swan eat and drink, eat and drink.

'If only she'd get up and move around,' sighed Mandy. 'How long do you think that will take, Dad?'

'I don't know, Mandy,' he replied. 'She's doing very well in other ways.'

'James and Simon thought they saw her move her injured wing a bit,' said Mandy.

'Mmm, I was just thinking that she seems to be holding it better,' Mr Hope nodded. 'As long as she's making this sort of progress, I don't really think we need worry. I reckon it might take a few days before she feels ready to get up.'

'So do you think her wing's going to be all right then?' Mandy asked eagerly. 'If you don't have to amputate it she'll be able to go back to the river when she's better and James and I will be able to visit her every day. It will be like having our own pet—' Mandy broke off when she noticed the look on Mr Hope's face. 'Dad! What's wrong?' she asked urgently.

'Mandy, love. Even if Sally doesn't have to lose her wing, I doubt she'll ever be able to fly properly again. I think the muscles and tendons are too badly damaged.' Mr Hope reached out and touched Mandy's hand.

'I'm sorry,' he went on softly, 'but in the end, Sally will have to go a bird sanctuary. It wouldn't be safe for her back on the river. The healthy swans and other birds might attack her. Even if they didn't, foxes would soon come to know she couldn't fly. That would encourage them to the river even more and they'd become an even greater hazard to the rest of the birdlife there, especially at nesting time.'

'You mean, Sally will never be able to go back to the river?'

'I'm afraid not, love,' said Mr Hope.

Mandy gazed sadly at Sally. The swan gazed back and made a little trumpeting noise. Mandy stood up and, with a deep sigh, walked quickly up the garden and into the house.

The next day Mandy was delighted when Elise phoned to ask if she could bring Maisy earlier than the time they'd arranged.

'Come over now, Elise!' said Mandy. 'Mum and Dad are going to give Sally a thorough check over. They want to examine her wing to make sure there's no sign of infection setting in. Helping you with Maisy will make the time pass quicker while I'm waiting for some news!'

'I'll come the back way,' said Elise. 'I'll let Maisy off her lead as soon as we're through the gate. If she sees you and runs to you, Mandy, try to stop her jumping up. Point to the ground like you did yesterday and see if she'll sit!'

Elise and Maisy's arrival went according to plan. Maisy caught sight of Mandy and bounded happily towards her.

Mandy bent slightly and held her arms out in front with her palms raised. Maisy skidded to a halt; Mandy stepped back and pointed to the ground.

Eyes bright, mouth open as though she were smiling, Maisy sat promptly.

'Well done! Good girl!' Mandy took the dog's face in her hands as she praised her.

'Watch this!' Elise walked slowly over to stand by Maisy's side. She ran her hand halfway down Maisy's back then pressed her fingers gently but firmly into the dog's backbone.

Maisy stood up and turned her head to look

up at Elise. Elise petted and praised her. 'Your swan gave me the idea of doing that to make Maisy stand,' she told Mandy. 'I tried it out when we got home yesterday. We've practised it a few times since then.'

'It's brilliant!' said Mandy, laughing as Maisy ran over to Sally's water bucket for a drink.

Elise smiled. 'That's why I phoned to see if we could come early,' she admitted. 'I was dying to show you our latest achievement. But what I'd really like to do, Mandy, is see if Maisy will react to the special whistle your mother told me about. The one only dogs can hear.'

'The silent whistle?' asked Mandy.

Elise nodded. 'I just bought one from the pet shop. I haven't tried it yet.'

'OK! What if I distract Maisy while you go to the other end of the garden?' suggested Mandy. 'Then you call me just before you blow the whistle and I'll watch Maisy to see if she hears it.'

Mandy went down on all fours and played a silly game with Maisy. After a couple of minutes Elise called Mandy's name. Of course the dog didn't react. Then Mandy watched the Dalmatian carefully. Maisy's ears went up; she lifted her head and looked all round. She'd heard the whistle!

'Do it again, Elise!' Mandy called excitedly. 'This time I'll get hold of her collar and we'll run to you!'

'Right!' called Elise. 'Now!' Again, Mandy watched Maisy carefully. Again, Maisy's ears pricked and she looked round. But Mandy didn't have time to get hold of Maisy's collar. The dog barked and streaked off . . . right up the garden . . . all the way to Elise!

Mandy followed as fast as she could; her eyes were full of tears. Tears were rolling down Elise's cheeks too, when Mandy reached her.

'She heard it! She really, really heard it!' laughed Elise, hugging first Maisy and then Mandy.

'And she seemed to know that it meant she was to come to you!' said Mandy.

At that moment, James arrived and Mandy had to explain all the excitement.

'Let's do it again to show James!' said Elise.

'Right! The two of us will distract Maisy. You go to the bottom of the garden, Elise,' said Mandy.

'Wow! She's a fast runner!' said James as Elise dashed off. Mandy nodded and bent down to rub Maisy's nose.

Just then Mr and Mrs Hope arrived at the

top of the garden, carrying Sally. Mandy heard them and glanced over her shoulder.

'Her wing's OK, Mandy!' Mrs Hope called reassuringly.

'Great!' Mandy called back. 'And, Mum! Maisy can hear the whistle. Elise will tell us when she's blowing it. Watch!'

The swan honked at the sound of Mandy's voice and struggled a bit. So Mr and Mrs Hope put her down.

'Now!' shouted Elise.

A couple of seconds later, Maisy turned and, tail wagging crazily, bounded down the garden to Elise. Laughing, James and Mandy ran after her.

'Mandy! James! Look!' shouted Mr Hope. 'Look at Sally!'

Mandy and James slowed and spun round. The swan was plodding slowly but determinedly down the garden.

'Sally!' Mandy cried joyfully. 'Oh, James, she's walking!'

Mandy and James started to walk towards her. The swan stopped, stretched out her neck and made a bubbly little whistling noise. Then she sank down.

'Don't go to her, Mandy!' Emily Hope called.

'Stand still. Try and get her to come to you.'

'Come on, Sally!' begged Mandy. 'Get up again, please get up again! Come on, Sally! Come on!'

Sally hissed loudly.

'Good swan!' James said encouragingly. 'Come to us!'

Sally lifted her head and circled it a couple of time; she honked and trumpeted, then she stretched her good wing. But she didn't get up.

'Maybe we should ask Elise to blow the whistle again,' said Mandy. 'I bet *that's* what made Sally get up.'

'Maybe it was,' James agreed. 'But it might confuse Maisy if Elise blows it again now. She couldn't know where to run to!'

'Pick Sally's water bucket up, Mandy!' called Mr Hope. 'She might come for a drink.'

Mandy moved to get it. 'Water, Sally,' she said. 'Come on, here's your bucket.' Mandy waved the bucket around a bit, then put it down.

The swan stretched her neck out and Mandy put her hand in the bucket and swished the water round. Sally blinked, folded her wing, rocked slightly and then . . .

'Oh, James!' said Mandy as Sally plodded quickly to her. 'It's worked.'

Sally honked; then moved faster until she reached the bucket. She was just about to dip her beak into it when Elise called a warning.

Maisy had slipped her collar and was running towards the bucket. She was there before James and Mandy had time to move!

The next second, the Dalmatian and the swan were side by side, both drinking out of the bucket. Everyone moved closer to watch; and to get Maisy out of Sally's way if they had to.

Sally was the first to stop drinking. Then Maisy, eyes on the swan, moved her head from the bucket. Sally stared at her with beady eyes, then tapped the ground with her bill. Maisy sat down, her mouth open in a doggy grin.

Sally honked, then plodded solemnly around Maisy in a large circle before going back to the bucket for another drink.

Elise moved forward, put Maisy's collar and lead on and looked round at the others, shaking her head in amazement. 'First they share a drink, then Sally points to the ground and Maisy sits! It's incredible!'

'This calls for a celebration,' said Emily Hope. 'How about iced lemonade and home-made biscuits all round?'

'And a doggy treat for Maisy!' said Mandy as

they all walked back up the garden.

'Bread for Sally, as well,' said James. 'And don't look now,' he added happily, 'but she's plodding along behind us!'

Eleven

'Right, Sally girl,' said Mandy, glancing up to the top of the garden. 'Simon's calling us. That means it's time for you to go in for your check-up. Come on. Stop watching my rabbits and follow me!'

Mandy picked up Sally's water bucket and started walking. She knew the swan would follow; over the past two weeks Sally had become very possessive about the red plastic bucket. For some reason she didn't like letting it out of her sight.

'It could be her big day, today!' said Simon, laughing as Sally raced up the garden after Mandy. 'I think she'll be getting a clean bill of health.'

'Mmm!' agreed Mandy, pulling a face. 'Mum and Dad are very pleased with the way her wing's healed. Oh, I'm glad really,' she said. 'But a clean bill of health means a bird sanctuary and I'll really miss her. I think the rabbits will, too!'

'I think Jean will miss Imogen's phone calls,' said Simon. 'She phones every day for the latest report on Sally, you know!'

Mandy smiled and turned to stroke the swan's head. 'Maisy will miss you too, won't she, Sally? They've become real good friends,' she added looking at Simon.

'Maisy seems to be getting on well enough with Blackie,' said Simon, pointing down the garden.

Mandy turned to see James and Elise being pulled through the gate by their dogs. 'It's Maisy's big day as well,' she told Simon. 'We're going to see if she'll obey hand signals even when there's another dog around.'

Mandy chuckled. 'Blackie was the obvious choice; he's sure to be a distraction!'

'Well, good luck!' laughed Simon, taking the bucket from Mandy. 'Come on, Sally. In we go.'

Mandy dashed off back down the garden. Maisy was sitting down but she was straining at her lead to get to Blackie, who seemed to be doing his best to get his lead tied round James's ankles!

'Hold your hand out, palm up, so Maisy can see it, Mandy!' said Elise. 'That's the signal for her to stay. That's it! It's worked!'

'Blackie's worse than usual today!' said James as Mandy helped to untangle the lead. 'Walter and Ernie were on the green when we came past, thatching the rushcart frame. Blackie ran over and started barking like crazy at it.'

'I think the frame looks just like a tent that's been covered with hay!' chuckled Elise. 'Blackie probably thinks it *is* a tent. He was barking to make whoever was inside it come out!'

'You're right, Elise,' said Mandy. 'It does look like a tent. But we'd better not let Walter or Ernie hear us saying so! There,' she added, 'that's you untangled, Blackie.'

'What do you want to do first, Elise?' asked James.

'Well, really, we've already done sit and stay,' said Elise, running her fingers down the centre of Maisy's back, then pausing to press gently against the Dalmatian's backbone.

'And that was stand!' said Mandy crouching in front of Maisy to praise her.

'I'd really like to try getting her to fetch!' said Elise. 'If you stay crouched down beside her, Mandy, with your right shoulder level with her head. I'll show Maisy her favourite rubber bone . . .' Elise pulled it from her pocket. 'I'll walk off with it and put it down. Then you thrust your left arm out and point at the bone. *If* she comes for it, I'll walk her back to you.'

The Dalmatian wasn't sure what was expected of her at first. When Mandy thrust her arm out and pointed, Maisy cocked her head on one side and looked puzzled.

But fetching was the one thing Blackie was good at. He kept fetching the rubber bone and placing it at Mandy's feet. Eventually, Maisy got the idea.

'I think Blackie's sorry he showed Maisy how to do it!' James chuckled after a few more goes. 'Maisy beats him to the bone every time now.'

'One more time then we'll give it a rest,' said Elise. 'It's best to stop before they get bored. Besides,' she added, looking up at the sky, 'it looks like it's going to pour with rain any minute.'

'Maybe we should go down to the green!' said James. 'Walter and Ernie will want to get the thatched frame covered with a tarpaulin. They'll be glad if we help, Mandy!'

'OK!' agreed Mandy. 'Just let me retie my laces. Blackie's been having a go at them! *And* he taught Maisy how to undo them!' she added, as the Dalmatian came over and tugged at a lace.

'Where did I put Blackie's lead?' asked James, looking round the garden.

'There is it!' Still crouching, Mandy pointed.

Maisy woofed and bounded off. She came back with Blackie's lead and put it down by Mandy's feet.

'Wow!' laughed Mandy, petting the dog. 'I

think that proves she's learned how to fetch! Clever dog, Maisy.'

'Leave Blackie with me, James,' Elise suggested when they got to her cottage. 'He'll only be in the way if you take him with you.'

'OK!' said James, clipping Blackie's lead on and passing it on Elise. 'Come on, Mandy. We might just make it before the rain.'

'How's that swan of yours?' asked Ernie once they'd managed to cover most of the rushcart with the huge waterproof sheet. He and Walter Pickard had seen Sally two or three times when they'd taken their own pets to Animal Ark.

'She's fine,' Mandy told him. 'Mum and Dad are as sure as they can be that she won't have to lose her wing. It hardly droops at all now, though she'll never be able to fly.'

'So she'll be off to a sanctuary soon then?' said Walter. 'I reckon you've all done a real good job there. You'll be sad to see her go!'

'Yes, but she's given us two very interesting weeks,' said James. 'I've written it all up for the Wildlife Watchers.'

'Here it comes,' said Ernie as the first huge drops of rain began to fall. 'We got the job done just in time. It doesn't look very attractive,' he said, scowling at the tall, covered shape. 'Looks a bit like a tent!'

Mandy and James hid a grin as Ernie went on, 'Still, if any of the judges arrive to do a spot check, I dare say they'll make allowances.'

'Of course they will!' said James. 'It's not finished yet.'

'The young sir's right, Ernie. Don't you go fretting,' said Walter, shaking his head as he looked at his old friend. 'Besides, there's plenty of pretty bits in the pond for the judges to see. Those plants that grew so mysteriously,' he chuckled throatily, 'are coming on a real treat. I don't think anyone will mention mermaids and suchlike at tomorrow's meeting. A bit more *natural* beauty like them, that's all that's needed.'

'You're right enough there, Walter,' agreed Ernie. 'Ponds are for living things, not fancy bits of plastic.'

An idea suddenly occurred to Mandy. A terrific, incredible and fabulous idea! 'Walter! Ernie! You're brilliant!' she shrieked, dancing around crazily. 'Absolutely brilliant! Ponds *are* for living things!'

'Uh-oh!' said James. 'I think I know what's coming next!'

'That's more'n I do,' grunted Ernie, scratching his head. 'But whatever it is, say it quickly, Mandy. We're getting soaked!'

'Sally's a living thing, isn't she!' laughed Mandy.

'Aye, and she's natural beauty all right,' said Walter, his face creasing into a smile. He'd grasped Mandy's meaning at once. 'Pond, grass, a big tree to shelter under, though perhaps she'd need a large wooden coop to go in at night. I reckon Ernie here could see to that!'

'Could you, Ernie? Would you?' asked James.

'Let me get this straight,' said Ernie. 'You're suggesting that our pond and our green would make a good home for the swan?'

'Yes!' Mandy and James spoke together.

'Aye, they would. And I agree!' said Walter.

'You go on back to Animal Ark, Mandy, and talk it over with your parents,' said Ernie. 'If they think it would be all right that's good enough for me. And I'll see to a coop. And now that's settled, can we go and get in out of this rain?'

'Come on, James!' Mandy started running. 'Leave Blackie at Elise's for now,' she said. 'I can't wait to see if Mum and Dad agree.'

* * *

'I don't see why Sally shouldn't live on the village pond,' said Mr Hope after Mandy and James had explained their idea. 'In fact,' he stroked his beard thoughtfully, 'there used to be a couple of swans on the pond when I was a lad. You'll have to put it to the rest of the village, though.'

'We will!' said Mandy, her eyes shining.

'At the meeting tomorrow,' added James. 'Walter and Ernie will back us up. They really seemed to like the idea. Ernie says he'll see to a coop for Sally.'

'Mum? *You've* not said anything yet!' Mandy gazed anxiously at her.

'We'd have to make sure that Sally uses the coop for shelter in bad weather and more importantly, at night-time as a protection from foxes,' said Mrs Hope. 'And uses it of her own accord,' she added firmly. 'I'm not having you running out every night to put her inside, Mandy!'

'Just the first couple of times to show her the idea,' bargained Mandy.

'OK!' Emily Hope smiled. 'Well then, as long as the villagers agree and as long as Sally settles down all right and uses what's provided for her, I think it's a great idea. The perfect solution!'

* * *

The following evening, the first part of the meeting went smoothly. Miss Davy wasted no time in reminding everybody of the ideas for the pond that had been suggested last time.

Even Mrs McFarlane and Flo Maynard voted for keeping the pond looking natural. 'It was like a sign, those plants suddenly growing in the pond,' said Flo. 'We just need a few more like them, that's all!'

Mrs Ponsonby snorted and said furiously, 'Suddenly growing there, my foot! Somebody *put* them there!'

'Well, somebody will be needed to put a few more there,' Walter Pickard said solemnly. 'I'd like to volunteer for that. Philip Meakin from the garden centre will sell us whatever we need at a reasonable price!' he added, winking at Mandy's gran. She'd already give him a list of plants and a price list supplied by Philip Meakin.

'And the sooner we get the job done, the better,' he continued. 'Final judging day is only just over a week away!'

'Thank you, Walter!' said Miss Davy. 'That's settled then. Now, I think everybody will have seen the posters regarding the rushcart procession and animal service! Everyone taking part to meet on the green at ten o'clock on the day! So, is there any other business?'

Mandy jumped to her feet. 'It isn't directly to do with the competition,' she said. 'But would anyone object if the swan we've been caring for at Animal Ark were to make her home on the pond?'

A soft murmur went through the crowd.

'Be nice, that would!' said Flo Maynard.

'Hear hear!' several people agreed loudly.

'A swan!' Mrs Ponsonby climbed on to her chair. 'Friends of the village!' she boomed, looking round the hall. 'It came as a great disappointment to me when you rejected my pretty and unusual idea of a bronze mermaid. However, I graciously accept your decision.' She bowed, nearly slipping off the chair. Regally regaining her balance, she continued, 'Now you *have* decided on plants for the pond . . . what . . . *what* would be the sense in having a swan on the pond? A swan who would *eat* the plants?'

'Cripes!' muttered James. 'How do we get out of that one?'

Elise Knight rose to her feet and looked shyly round. 'Mandy has had the swan out in Animal Ark's garden every day since she rescued her,' she said. 'Why don't we ask Mandy if the swan has eaten any of the flowers there?'

'Well, Mandy?' asked Miss Davy.

'The only thing Sally nibbled at were some dandelions,' said Mandy. 'And seeing as they shouldn't have been growing in Dad's lawn anyway . . .' Mandy gave a mischievous smile, '. . . Sally did us a favour!'

'So those of us living *in* the village itself . . .' Walter Pickard glanced at Mrs Ponsonby, who lived in Bleakfell Hall, an enormous house off one of the moorland roads above the village. '. . . I take it we're in favour of having the swan on our pond, on our green?'

'Hear, hear!' shouted the willing supporters.

'Well, don't say I didn't warn you!' said Mrs Ponsonby. But she knew she was beaten. Shaking her head, she allowed two burly farm-hands to help her down from the chair.

Mandy and James hurried away after the meeting. They wanted to make plans for taking Sally to the pond.

'We can't just take her and leave her there,' Mandy said thoughtfully. 'We need to get her used to the idea slowly.'

James nodded. 'Let's take her down for a little while tomorrow. Do you think she'll follow us all the way?'

Mandy nodded. 'All we need do is to carry her red bucket! She's sure to follow us then.'

Mandy was right. The next morning Sally marched happily along behind her and James, her beady eyes on the bucket Mandy was carrying.

'I hope no one comes up to talk to us,' said Mandy as they got close to the green. 'We don't want any distractions for a while.'

'We'll probably be OK,' said James, glancing round.

Mandy nodded. Now the pond was in sight she felt worried and excited at the same time. Sally was looking around with interest. And when she honked loudly, Mandy smiled. 'She's seen the water,' she said. 'Haven't you, Sally? Come on, you'll soon be having a lovely swim!'

But when they reached the pond, Sally sank down onto the grass, and when Mandy crouched down beside her, the swan wound her neck firmly around Mandy's and made her funny little crying noise.

'Oh, heck!' said James, shoving his glasses further on to his nose. 'I think she's frightened, Mandy.'

'Maybe she remembers being in the Parker Smythes' swimming-pool,' sighed Mandy, managing to move Sally's neck from hers. 'What can we do, James? How can we stop her feeling frightened?'

James sat down and took off his trainers and socks. 'There's only one thing for it. *I'll* get in the pond to show her it's OK. And I'll take the bucket in, too!'

He got in and started jumping around and splashing. 'See, Sally, It's nice, it's *sss*uper,' he hissed encouragingly. Then he flapped his arms up and down, as though they were wings. 'Come on – come to James!' he said.

Sally hissed and trumpeted then stretched her neck out a bit. James trumpeted back and Mandy burst out laughing. James ignored her laughter and continued flapping and trumpeting. Sally kept darting her neck out towards James and then started making paddling movements with her enormous feet.

By now, Mandy was laughing so hard, she got a stitch in her side. 'Oh, stop it, you two!' she gasped, bending over to try and relieved the stitch. 'Please stop!'

Neither Mandy nor James noticed the well-dressed lady approaching. Sally saw her, though, and promptly put her long neck over Mandy's shoulders and looked mournfully at the newcomer.

'Cripes!' muttered James, blushing violently as he suddenly caught sight of the stranger. He grabbed the bucket and climbed clumsily out of the pond. But he slipped in the mud on the steep bank and stumbled forward. The bucket flew out of his hand and shot towards the stranger.

'Gosh! I'm sorry,' James gasped. Not only had the bucket almost hit the lady, but water from inside the bucket had sprayed her pretty summery dress!

'We were trying to encourage the swan to get in,' Mandy explained. 'My parents are vets, and we've been looking after the swan because she hurt her wing. Didn't you, Sally?' she added, rubbing the top of the swan's head. Sally looked at Mandy and made her little crying noise over and over again.

'We'll have to get her back to Animal Ark, James,' said Mandy, tenderly stroking Sally's neck. 'Don't cry like that, Sally,' she begged. 'Everything will be all right, I promise.'

Sally nuzzled her beak into Mandy's hair and hissed mournfully. 'Come on,' Mandy said gently. 'We're going home, Sally.'

James apologised again to the stranger who smiled and bent to pick up his trainers and socks. 'I should put these on before you walk

anywhere,' she told him. And then, she walked away across the green.

James bundled his socks into his wet pocket and thrust his feet into his trainers. Then he hurried to catch up with Mandy and Sally. Now they were leaving the pond area, Sally seemed to be happy enough. But she hissed crossly when Mrs Ponsonby marched up to them.

'I saw that unfortunate episode, James Hunter,' she said, her chins wobbling with rage. 'That was a competition judge you threw the bucket at! Welford will never win now! And all because of that swan!'

James felt terrible. He muttered another apology then trotted after Mandy. 'Mrs Ponsonby could be right for once,' he said gloomily. 'Welford *won't* win now, not after what I just did!'

'And it looks as though we won't have Sally on the pond, either,' said Mandy, just as gloomily. 'We've ruined the village's chance of winning and Sally will have to go to a bird sanctuary after all!'

They took the back route to Animal Ark. When Mandy opened the wooden gate at the end of the garden, Sally pushed her way through first. Then, her enormous feet scarcely touching the ground, she made her way to the annexe door trumpeting loudly all the time.

'Someone's glad to be back,' said Simon, opening the door to see what all the noise was about, and smiling when Sally walked in and went straight to her cage. 'You look wetter than Sally, James. Did she splash you when she got in the pond?'

'It was no good, Simon,' Mandy said despondently, going on to tell him the sorry tale. 'And look at her,' she sighed, pointing to Sally. 'She usually needs loads of persuasion to go into her cage. Now she looks as if she's settled there for good!'

'Don't tell me you two are giving up on the idea after only one try,' said Simon. 'This isn't the Mandy and James I'm used to!'

'Oh, we're not going to give up!' Mandy said, suddenly feeling determined. 'Let's have another try after evening surgery.'

James grinned up at Simon. 'I knew she'd soon get her fighting spirit back,' he said. 'Then he dodged away as Mandy made to punch him on his shoulder.

'Why don't you give Sally less food than usual at six o'clock,' suggested Simon. 'And—'

'And take some bread to throw in the pond!' interrupted Mandy. 'We can put it in her bucket. That's a brilliant idea, Simon!'

'Sure is,' agreed James. 'It might save me from having to go in the water again! But I think I can improve on that idea. When we get near the pond, how about dropping pieces of bread behind us? Sally will be so busy keeping her beak to the ground, following the trail, she might follow it into the pond without thinking!'

At six-thirty, James and Mandy were on their way again with Sally padding along quite happily behind them.

'It's a good job the rushcart's at the opposite end from the pond,' said Mandy as they got close to the green. 'Look, James, there's quite a little crowd there.'

'Yes!' said James. 'I think it's finished at last. Right, I'm going to start dropping the bread now, Mandy.'

The swan looked like a living vacuum cleaner as she scurried along, neck down, beak to the ground, sucking up the pieces as soon as they were dropped. Soon, they were close to the pond.

'If we stand together, right at the edge, and drop some bread right behind us . . .' said James.

'Hopefully Sally will nudge us out of the way looking for more,' Mandy finished. 'Then we'll throw a couple of pieces into the water, just out of her reach . . .'

'And move apart quickly,' James grinned.

The first part of the plan worked perfectly. Sally gobbled the bread from behind James and Mandy's heels, then tapped them smartly on their legs. They sprang apart sideways and Sally moved forward. Then she stopped and drew her chest and body back. Then . . .

Mandy grabbed hold of James's arm and held her breath. For a few seconds Sally teetered and rocked; she moved one enormous foot forward, then the other and . . .

'She's done it! She's in!' gasped Mandy. 'James, look, she's diving just like the ducks do.'

'Up-ending,' James said hoarsely, his eyes shining behind his glasses.

'And now she's swimming towards the middle!' said Mandy. 'Come on, James, let's run to the other side and see if she'll swim all the way across.'

'We're about to get an audience,' said James, peering across the green at the three figures moving away from the rushcart.

'It's OK,' said Mandy. 'It's Walter, Ernie and

Grandad. Sally knows them.'

Sally was still in the middle of the pond when they arrived. 'Holding one foot up on her back,' noted Walter Pickard. 'Look to me like she's well settled there.'

They stood for a while longer watching. Apart from up-ending a few times more, Sally didn't make any attempt to swim closer to them. She didn't even react when Mandy called her.

'Come on over and take a look at the rushcart, Mandy love,' Grandad suggested gently. 'Leave the swan on her own for a while and see what happens.'

'All right,' Mandy agreed with a sigh. 'I know it's silly,' she admitted, as they started moving away. 'I mean, we *want* Sally to make the pond and the green her home. But . . .' Her voice trailed away and she glanced back over her shoulder. Sally hadn't moved.

'But we didn't mean it to happen so quickly,' said James, shoving his glasses roughly into place.

'Wild creatures know their own minds,' said Walter. 'If it feels right, she'll stop there in the water. You leave her to it. We'll be sitting outside the Fox and Goose for most of the evening. We'll give you a ring if you're needed.'

Mandy glanced at James and he nodded. 'OK, Walter!' said Mandy.

'There's my girl,' whispered Grandad, squeezing her arm.

'Now then,' said Walter. 'What d'you think of the rushcart now the thatching's finished? I reckon we've done a grand job, even though I say it myself.'

'It's terrific!' said James, walking round and examining it carefully. The frame stood nearly three metres high. 'It'll look really tall when it's been lifted on to the cart.'

'I can hardly wait to see the procession of animals following it to the church,' said Mandy.

'You've only got just over a week to wait, Mandy,' said Grandad. 'It will be here soon enough.'

'Well, right now,' said Mandy, 'I'm going home. Before I change my mind,' she added with a last lingering look towards the pond, where Sally seemed happily settled.

Twelve

'I know you said having the swan on the pond wasn't anything to do with the competition, Mandy,' said Mrs McFarlane, 'but somehow she makes the village seem friendlier! Folk gather round the pond to chat now there's something to see. Perhaps the judges have been by and noticed that!'

A week had passed since the evening Sally had decided to stay on the pond, and she'd settled down really well.

'She acts as if the pond and the green have been her home all her life,' Mandy said happily. 'But I think people gather round the pond to look at the plants as well. The ones that grew *mysteriously*,' Mandy chuckled, '*and* the new ones!'

'Well, there'll be plenty of people from other villages looking at everything tomorrow!' said Mrs McFarlane. 'They're sure to come well before the announcement!'

Mandy nodded. 'I couldn't believe it when I heard!' she said. 'Fancy the judges wanting to announce the winning village *here*! Right after our rushcart procession!'

'Makes sense really!' said Walter Pickard who'd come for some stamps. 'All the other villages have had their ceremonies. The points for the rushcarts are added to points awarded from the spot checks. So *their* points will have all been added up.'

'I don't know if it's a good thing or a bad thing us being the last village with the rushcart!' Mrs McFarlane pursed her lips as she counted out Walter's change.

'Well, none of the other villages had a procession of animals ending in a special service for them as part of their ceremony!' said Mandy. 'That's sure to make ours stand out!'

'Maybe that's what I'm worried about,' said Mrs McFarlane. 'It's a lovely idea, Mandy and I'm bringing my Billy in his new cage. But, let's face it . . . not all the animals will be as easy to control as my budgie. Almost anything could happen!'

As soon as she woke next morning, Mandy leaped out of bed and ran to the window to check the weather. 'Oh, no!' she groaned, staring up at the two black and angry-looking clouds. 'It can't rain! It *can't!*'

She showered, dressed quickly and hurried downstairs. 'Have you *seen* the weather?' she said, dashing into the kitchen. 'It isn't funny!' she added as her parents looked at each other and smiled.

'Grandad's just phoned,' Adam Hope explained. 'He'd knew you'd be in a panic. He said to tell you not to worry. He says the clouds are just passing over and it will be bright and sunny within the hour.'

An hour and a half later Mandy had groomed her rabbits, fastened the reed collars Flo Maynard had made for them round their necks and was flying down the back lane to meet James on the green. Grandad had been right; the clouds were gone and it was indeed bright and sunny.

As Mandy ran past the cottages she saw Ernie,

Elise and Walter in their gardens grooming their pets. She waved and called a greeting to all of them, but she didn't stop. She'd be seeing them again very soon!'

As Mandy turned the corner, she heard Mrs Ponsonby's voice. 'No, no, Pandora! Come to Mumsy-Wumsy, my precious. You'll catch some sort of terrible disease if you play with the rubbish bin! Toby, Toby! Oh, you terrible boy!'

Mandy laughed as Mrs Ponsonby's dogs pounced on, growled at and tried to get out the contents of the rubbish bin on the village green.

'It isn't funny, Mandy!' scolded Mrs Ponsonby, teetering after her dogs in high-heeled shoes that kept sinking into the grass.

'And why have you brought that awful plastic bucket?' she panted. 'I do hope you're not thinking of carrying it in the procession. That's exactly why I came early, to make sure nobody lowers the tone of things! Unless it's for . . .' Mrs Ponsonby stood still and beamed alarmingly at Mandy.

'Why, of course. It's for putting little accidents in! What a thoughtful girl you are! Ah, here are my little preciouses. They always come when Mumsy-Wumsy calls them! It's a good job, too. Here's James and he's with Lydia. She's got a nasty, smelly billy-goat with her! I'll take Pandora and Toby to sit with me on the bench.'

'Good idea,' said Mandy thankfully. She grinned at James and Lydia, petted Houdini the goat, then turned as she heard a farm vehicle drawing up.

'It's the Gills,' said James. 'With two chubby piglets as well as Maggie and Harry.'

'James!' shouted Angela. 'I've brought Harry's babies, too. They're all snuggled together in the bedroom bit of the cage!'

After that, everyone seemed to arrive at once. They brought cats, rabbits, mice, rats, hamsters and guinea-pigs in all sorts of decorated boxes, baskets and cages. There were three calves, a few sheep, two ponies and a foal, dogs of all shapes and sizes, two parrots, budgerigars, canaries and goldfish in bowls.

Mandy's parents and Simon had arrived; each carrying one of Mandy's rabbits in a cosy sling strapped across their chests. They were talking to Ernie Bell who'd brought Tiddles in a cat basket and Sammy the squirrel on his shoulder.

Duke the shire horse was ready between the shafts of the cart. Mrs Ponsonby had removed herself from the bench and, shouting to make herself heard above the barking, squealing, mooing, baa-ing and other noises, was bossily trying to organise everybody into a line behind the rushcart.

'Here's Mum and Dad with Eric,' said James. 'I think I'll leave Blackie with them while we go and fetch Sally.'

Mandy nodded. 'Elise is already walking Maisy towards the pond,' she said. 'I'm sure Sally will get out when she sees Maisy *and* the bucket!'

As they dashed towards the pond, Mandy went on, 'Mrs Ponsonby thinks I brought the bucket to put little accidents in! I didn't dare tell her I'd brought it to make Sally follow us! After all, Sally deserves to be part of the procession, too.'

'I hope you two are safe with that bucket today!' The well-dressed judge whom James had splashed while trying to get Sally into the pond, smiled as she hurried past towards the rushcart.

'It's for persuading Sally to join the procession,' Mandy called happily. 'She always follows whoever carries it.'

'Well, she always used to,' James murmured as they got close to the pond. 'Let's hope she still does!'

Sally obviously remembered the bucket and Maisy. She swam quickly to the edge of the pond, climbed on a large boulder and on to the grass. She hissed and honked at Maisy and pointed her bill to the ground.

'Oh, no! *I* didn't want you to sit Maisy!' laughed Elise, running her hand down Maisy's back and pressing her fingers against the dog's spine to make her stand up again.

'Come on, Sally! The procession's moving! Follow us!' said Mandy, waving the bucket. And they all hurried back across the green to tag on the end of the procession behind Christopher and Lola Gill and the two young piglets.

'Yip-yip-yip!' said Lola. 'Keep up with the rest! Oh, look!' she added with a giggle. 'Here's that funny lady with the dog that looks like a piglet!'

'Sweet little things!' cooed Mrs Ponsonby. 'Keep in line, now. Keep in line. What is it, my precious?' she asked Pandora. She was holding the wriggling, whining dog under one plump arm.

'She wants to walk with the pig twins. They'll look like triplets then!' said Christopher. 'Come on, piggy-dog!' He stretched up and pulled Pandora out of Mrs Ponsonby's arms.

'Mrs Ponsonby! Mrs Ponsonby!' yelled someone from the front of the procession. '*Could* you get your Toby? He's frightening my rats!'

'Rats!' shrieked Mrs Ponsonby.

That did it! Mrs Ponsonby's shrill cry excited several dogs into action. They pulled away from their owners and darted here, there and everywhere, barking and yelping as they spotted imaginary rats under hedges, up trees or over garden walls!

All the extra activity excited Sally. She stretched her long neck and reached up to pull at Mrs Ponsonby's cartwheel hat. It fell to the ground. One young piglet picked it up and, followed by its squealing twin, charged away with it.

There were screams and cries as the piglets dived through the crowd in between legs and around ankles!

'Yip-yip-yip!' yelled Lola and Christopher. 'Come on, piggy-dog. Let's catch them!'

Pandora had never run so fast in her life as she merrily followed the twins and the piglets.

'Cripes! We'll never get to the church at this rate!' said James, bending down to scoop up a Jack Russell.

It was a good ten minutes before any sort of order was restored. But after that nothing untoward happened and, at last, the procession reached the churchyard!

Reverend Hadcroft was waiting to greet them. His cat, Jemima, was sitting on the bench in the church porch. 'I couldn't persuade her to get into her cat box,' he said. 'She'll have to take part from there!'

'Duke can take part from the railings over there!' said Dan Venables, unhitching the big shire horse. 'I'll tether him and get him a drink of water from the churchyard tap. Oh, heck!' he added, 'I've forgotten to bring a bucket!'

'It's OK, Dan. I've got one!' Mandy made her way to the front of the cart and gave Dan the red plastic bucket.

She turned to go back to James, Elise, Maisy and Sally then decided it would be too much of an effort. She was hemmed in by Butch, Flo Maynard's huge dog, Houdini the goat and two calves. Then Christopher and Lola tugged her arm and asked her if she'd hold the piglets. 'They keep getting trodden on and then they squeal and upset the other animals!' Lola explained.

The vicar faced his unusual congregation and spoke only a few words before asking everyone to join in the hymn All things bright and beautiful, All creatures great and small.

But at that point Dan Venables grabbed

Mandy's arm and said urgently, 'You'd better do something about that swan. She's making her way over to Duke. He'll kick out at her, Mandy. The one thing he turns nasty with is swans!'

Dan tried to make his way through the crowd, but although the humans moved willingly, the animals only managed to hinder him.

Mandy looked round in panic; she was hemmed in *and* she had two piglets in her arms. But she knew James and Elise were somewhere at the back of the crowd.

'James! Elise! Get Maisy to fetch Sally!' she yelled. Then she unloaded the piglets into the nearest empty arms she spotted – the well-dressed judge's – and ducked and dived her way after Dan.

Mandy managed to get through quicker than Dan; skirting the outside of the crowd, she spotted Duke. Sally was just a couple of metres away from him. But Maisy was racing towards the swan. Those who realised what was happening were shouting encouragement; they didn't realise the Dalmatian couldn't hear them!

And now, Maisy had reached Sally. She started prancing round her and . . . Mandy let out a huge sigh of relief. James and Elise were almost there.

Thanks to Maisy slowing the swan down as she tried her best to 'fetch' her, Elise and James were in time. James grabbed the red bucket from Duke's side, patted the horse quickly and dashed back to Sally.

Sally hissed and honked as James put the bucket down.

'The Dalmatian saved the swan!' yelled someone in the crowd while Dan Venables calmed Duke, who was straining at his tether.

Then an awed silence fell as, side by side, Sally and Maisy dipped into the bucket for a drink.

Through the mist in her eyes, Mandy saw Reverend Hadcroft walking towards them. For a long moment, he gazed at the swan and the dog. Then he turned to face the crowd and led them into the words of the hymn.

Everyone had tears in their eyes when the singing came to an end. Then the vicar asked everyone to make their way back to the green to hear the competition results announced.

'In spite of not having a mermaid statue, if only you hadn't soaked one of the judges, James, and you hadn't thrust the piglets upon her, Mandy, we just might have won the competition,' said Mrs Ponsonby as everyone started to make their way out through the lych-gate. 'And all because of . . .' she glared at Sally. '. . . all because of this swan!'

Sally gave a small hiss and lowered her long, white neck to nibble at the flowered buckles on Mrs Ponsonby's shoes. 'And it *does* eat flowers!' she added crossly. 'What did I tell you?'

The farm animals were taken back to their trailers which were parked in the Fox and Goose's carpark, then everyone gathered on the green around the platform which had been put in place by the competition organisers.

There were three judges on the platform. Mandy groaned when she saw the dirty marks on the lady judge's white blouse. If only she'd chosen someone else to give the piglets to!

One judge stepped forward and gave a short speech about all the villages that had taken part in the competition. He concluded, 'It was very hard to choose the winner. We found all the villages friendly, attractive and well-cared for. There wasn't one rushcart that deserved more points than another. And although today's ceremony, here in Welford, stood out for obvious reasons . . .' he paused for strained laughter, '. . . the more traditional ceremonies were just as good in their own way! However, we *do* have a winner.' The judge paused again; but not for long.

He smiled down at the crowd then said loudly and clearly, 'One village won by twenty points. The exact number of points awarded to two of that village's young folk who showed such a caring attitude to . . .' He glanced down at his notes, then continued, '. . . to Sally, the swan who lives on the pond here on Welford's village green!'

The cheers rang out and Mandy turned to pet Sally who, of course, was standing next to her.

'All because of this swan; just like I told you!' said Mrs Ponsonby, as she stepped graciously over to join the villagers in congratulating Mandy and James.

'Attention, please!' shouted the judge. And when everyone was silent he said, 'Now, all that's left for me to do is to ask Mandy, James and, of course, Sally to step forward and accept the trophy!'

The next edition of the *Dales News* bore the headline SWAN IN THE SWIM! It was followed by the full story, retold from the notes James had made for the Welford Wildlife Watchers, and there were three photographs. One of Mandy, James and Sally receiving the trophy, one of Sally swimming in the pond and one of Maisy and Sally drinking together from the bucket. That picture was entitled 'Best Friends in the "Friendliest Village" in North Yorkshire'.

'They've got it a bit wrong,' Mandy said to James when they saw the newspaper. 'Welford's the friendliest village in the *world*!'

If you like Animal Ark then you'll love the RSPCA's Animal Action Club! Anyone aged 13 or under can become a member for just £5.50 a year. Join up and you can look forward to six issues of Animal Action magazine – each one is bursting with animal news, competitions, features, posters and celebrity interviews. Plus we'll send you a special membership card, badge and stickers. There are all sorts of fun things to do as well!

To be really animal-friendly just complete the form – a photocopy is fine – and send it, with a cheque or postal order for £5.50 made payable to the RSPCA, to Animal Action Club, RSPCA, Causeway, Horsham, West Sussex RH12 1HG. We'll send you a membership pack and your first copy of *Animal Action*.

Registered charity no 219099

Don't delay, join today!

Name ....

Address ....

....

.... **Postcode** ....

Date of Birth ....

Youth membership of the Royal Society for the Prevention of Cruelty to Animals

AACHOD